JULIE'S HERITAGE

JULIE'S HERITAGE

by

CATHERINE MARSHALL

Decorations by E. HARPER JOHNSON

DAVID McKAY COMPANY, INC.

NEW YORK

JULIE'S HERITAGE

COPYRIGHT © 1957

BY CATHERINE MARSHALL

PUBLISHED SIMULTANEOUSLY IN THE DOMINION OF CANADA

FIRST EDITION MARCH 1957
REPRINTED JANUARY 1958
SEPTEMBER 1958
OCTOBER 1962
NOVEMBER, 1964
MARCH, 1967

LIBRARY OF CONGRESS CATALOG CARD NUMBER 57-7092

Printed in the United States of America

163093

The author wishes to express her gratitude to Mrs. Augusta Baker of the New York Public Library for her help and advice; to Mr. Herbert L. Wright of the N.A. A.C.P. for his counsel; to the Juilliard School of Music for providing background material; and to those men, women and young people who offered the benefit of their experience.

C. M.

To
my niece
TERRY SUE

1

JULIE JUMPED OFF THE BUS AND STARTED UP THE LONG twisting stairway that led from the street to her house on the hillside. But soon her feet began to drag and the dress box felt heavy in her hand. She wondered again why Mother had sent her to get a new dress. She already had a closet full of dresses bought in nearby New York in happy anticipation of her new adventure, her first year in high school. Did Mother sense her agonized waiting? Or worse, did she think that Bets and Doris would never call?

Oh, it couldn't be, not after all their years together. Why, Julie could scarcely remember a time when they had not been an inseparable threesome, Bets Hampton, Doris Regan and Julie Brownell. There must be some good reason why they hadn't phoned. Bets had prolonged her visit to her grandmother. The Regans had stayed on at their cottage at the lake. This afternoon, tonight maybe, they would get in touch with her and tomorrow the three of them would swing off to school arm in arm, as they always had. They might even have called while she **was** downtown. Julie began to hurry again.

At the last turn in the stairway she stopped dead in her tracks, startled, almost frightened at the sight of the boy who sat on the steps of the porch. She saw first the great bulk of him and his big round head, so dark against the light-gray boards of the house. But then she ran toward him with a glad cry. "George!"

It was only her cousin after all and she forgot her aunt's eyes, red-rimmed from weeping, and the whispers not meant for her ears that George had "gone bad." For this was the well-loved friend of her childhood, her playmate, protector and ally, and she had not seen him for three years.

"George!" she repeated and the welcome rang in her rich young voice.

" 'Lo, Julie." When he stood up, he towered above her and his wide shoulders shut out the familiar sight of the garden so that she could only look up into his sullen un-smiling face. Sudden fear choked her again. Something must be wrong or why was he here, after staying away for so long?

"Mother!" she said hoarsely. "Where's Mother?"

"Inside. Busy, I guess. It's you I came to see."

But Julie was not reassured. "I'll be back," she said. She flew up the steps and banged through the screen door, calling her mother as she ran. Her panic was shot through with guilt. It was her fault if something had happened to Mother. For she had wished her parents harm, blaming them for the silent phone as if its rebuff were to them and not her.

"In the kitchen, Julie." Mother sounded calm enough,

but she always did. Julie had never heard her raise her voice for any reason at all. Besides, what was she doing in the kitchen? Where was Sarah Lou?

Sarah Lou was there too. Julie stopped in the doorway and the everyday sights and sounds in the room quieted her apprehension. Sarah Lou's plump body bulged over the table, and peas fell with little plops from the pods in her hands into the pan before her. Mother must have had one of her urges to bake. Her trim figure was partly covered with a starchy apron and the electric mixer whirred and hummed at her side.

"Did you find a pretty dress?" she asked.

"Yes, Mother. Navy blue." Julie set the box on a chair and twisted its paper-string handle on her finger.

Sarah Lou flashed her strong white teeth. "Your mamma's making you a devil's food."

Devil's food. Her favorite cake. Another thrust of sympathy. Julie's eyes moved from Sarah Lou to Mother and back to the box on the chair. How could her mother possibly know? Julie had kept her mouth firmly shut, made secretive by a new-born shame.

The string around her finger was so tight that it hurt, but she forced her voice to be casual. "Anyone call?"

"No, dear, but George is here. Didn't you see him on the porch?"

"Yes. I saw him." Nearly five o'clock on the day before the start of school and still they had not called!

"Wouldn't you like to invite him to dinner?"

"George?" But his name had been almost taboo in this house ever since he had joined that hoodlum gang.

"Why, I think it would be nice. Don't you?" There was an artificial ring in Mother's tone, as if the words were a paper wrapper to cover the meaning hidden within them. A puzzled frown creased Julie's forehead until their import struck her like a blow. Accept him. He's your cousin. We're in this together.

"I'll ask him." She turned and started back to the porch. But she could not walk away from her thoughts. Mother knew how it was for her because she, too, had suffered, she and George and everyone like them. Scenes scarcely noticed, quickly forgotten, ran through her mind. Mother between her and a too indifferent salesgirl; between her and an embarrassed greeting on the street. And long before that, a boy with a sneer on his face and a taunt on his lips. What was the word with which he had mocked them? Julie could not remember it now. She had been too young to know what it meant.

George was pacing up and down in front of the house, his hands in his pockets.

Julie sat down on the top step. "I'm sorry I made you wait."

"Not many people make me wait." George punctuated his boast with a toss of his head.

"Well, I'm sorry!" Her words rose toward a peak of

hysteria. There was a kind of menace in this big thick-set fellow, a stranger after all.

He stopped his pacing abruptly and looked at her with curiosity. Then he plumped himself down on a step below her so that all she could see was the top of his woolly head.

"Listen, Julie. Listen. I suppose you think it's funny, me coming around after all this time."

"Mother would like you to stay for dinner." Suddenly, Julie did not want to know why he had come.

George ignored her invitation. "See, I know you're starting high school tomorrow and I just wanted to tell you, you don't need to take anything from anybody. See?"

"What do you mean, George?" She leaned toward him, her heart pounding strangely.

"It may be all right for you. Your old man's a doctor, sort of someone in this town in spite of—of everything." He had become uncertain and his feet scraped back and forth along the walk.

"I don't know what you mean." But she did. And she knew, as she actually had all along, why Bets and Doris had stayed away. And why she had shrunk from calling them.

George whipped around to face her and his scowl was angry. "I mean, you don't need to let anyone bother you. You just tell 'em you're George Thompson's cousin." His forehead smoothed out and a malicious grin widened his lips. "They're all afraid of me down at school."

For a moment she was afraid herself, for there was an

odd gleam in his eyes. Then she remembered his old ten-
derness toward all things smaller than himself and she almost laughed. "George Thompson! How could anyone
be afraid of you?"

He was angry again and he stood up and glared down
at her. "They're afraid of me because I'm tough. And I
don't care what anyone thinks, not even my own family,
not even you, Julie. Only you're my cousin and I'm not
going to let anyone hurt you. See?"

"I see."

"Okay, then. Good luck, kid." A small smile flickered
over his face before he pulled away and started down the
stairs.

When he had disappeared around the bend in the stairway, Julie stretched out one arm, and nearly called out
after him. Perhaps at the first he, too, had been abandoned
by friends. Maybe he could tell her what to do. For she
would give anything, anything at all, to change this sharp-
edged pain to anger.

No! No! No! It simply could not happen to her. George
had admitted her father's good name. But more than that
was the strength of her friendship, firm and secure over all
these years. Always and always, there had been the three
of them, Bets Hampton, Doris Regan and Julie Brownell.
Surely she would hear from them tonight.

When the phone did ring during dinner, Julie could
not move to answer it. Numbed by the fear that it was not
they, she sat perfectly still, her hand clasped tightly around

the handle of her fork. There was an endless pause before her father said, "I'll get it. It's probably for me, anyway."

Julie sat stiff and listening, like a fawn who catches the crackle of a hunter's feet in the leaves of the forest. Her father's voice seemed to come from far off. "Oh yes, Mrs. Reynolds. How is Willie tonight?"

Mrs. Reynolds! Don't cry, Julie. Don't cry! She laid her fork carefully on her plate and lowered her lids over her stinging eyes.

The faraway voice gave some brief instructions and ended on a note of reassurance. "I'll be there in half an hour."

As if there were an illness in this house, too, Mother's tone echoed his encouragement. "Julie, high school will be fun. You'll learn new things, make new friends . . ."

New friends—when all she wanted was the old. She was aware that her father passed her and of the soft swish of his chair on the rug as he reseated himself at the table.

"I'm worried about Willie Reynolds," he said. "I'd better get down there right away. Mother, do you mind if I skip dessert?"

Before Mother could answer, Julie heard her own voice, low but unmistakably clear. "Oh, let him die."

The words fell into a shocked silence, and Julie herself shared in the horror of what she had said. Her ears caught the sound of Mother's sucked-in breath, and prickles broke out all over her skin.

But her father sensed that she didn't really wish for Willie to die, but had only uttered her own despair. He spoke kindly. "Julie, there are hard times in everyone's life. But they pass. They do pass."

Julie cried out in bitter denial. "They don't pass. They can't. Not for us. Look at George."

Her father turned away from her toward her mother, his brows raised in a wordless question. Julie saw the sorrow on her mother's face and the almost imperceptible nod of her head. Then her father began to talk again and his words were measured and slow.

"Julie, I guess the time has come when you must be truly one of our people."

"And never see Doris or Bets again?" She had not meant to say their names.

"Let them see you in a clearer light."

"How can I?" she wondered. They knew her so well.

"You can live so that they can see your worth. This is the way our fathers before us have brought us so far toward our place among men. But there is still a long road ahead, and you and I must carry on. For this is the Negro heritage. This we must do for our children's children."

Children's children! How could she care? This was now, and she was herself. She was the one who ached for her friends. The ache was stronger than knowledge, stronger than fear, and the pull of it was so powerful that she could not let them go.

And so in the morning, she ran down the long stairway

that separated her house from those on the street below. In the bright warmth of the early fall, with the skirt of her new dress swishing around her legs, she could almost recapture the excitement of her anticipation. High school! All summer she had dreamed of this day; over and over she had pictured each detail, so that when she rounded the curve that brought the Regans' house into view, she fully expected to see Doris waiting, as she had in the dream.

But Doris was not there. A maroon car stood in front of the house, a car something like the Hamptons', only not as new and shining. Julie's eyes saw it pull away from the curb but she scarcely noticed. All of her mind was focused on the force of her will. Let Doris be home. Let Doris be home.

Yet when she reached the house, she could not make herself step up and ring the bell. She stood on the sidewalk, torn between hope and dread, until the door opened without her ring and she leaned toward it, hardly able to breathe. But it was not Doris who stepped onto the porch. It was Mrs. Regan, gaunt as ever, with a faded bandanna tied over her curlers and a broom and a small rug in her hands.

Julie let out her breath. The appearance of Mrs. Regan had given her a little stay, and the familiar sight of her made everything seem unchanged. She greeted her eagerly. "Hello, Mrs. Regan."

Mrs. Regan's head twitched toward Julie and a bright patch of color flared up in each of her cheeks. "Oh, hello,

Julie." She dropped the rug onto the porch and took a few swipes at it with her broom.

She's busy, Julie told herself. She's always like this. If I ask about Doris—if I ask about Doris . . . "Did you have a nice summer?"

Mrs. Regan went on with her work. "Just the same as usual, Julie. Cooking, cleaning, washing, ironing. In the country or here, it's the same for me."

"Oh," Julie said. Where is Doris? Where is she?

The movement of the broom slowed to a stop. "Julie, hadn't you better . . ." Mrs. Regan glanced at her once and lines of worry wrinkled her face. Then she began to sweep with more vigor than ever and her words tumbled out to keep pace with her broom. "Well, I suppose you're anxious about starting high school. I guess all the girls are. I know Doris is. Why, she was in such a hurry this morning, she couldn't wait for anybody or anything. Hardly ate a mouthful of breakfast. I told her, 'You can't start out on an empty stomach.' But do you think she would listen to me?"

"You mean she's—gone?"

Mrs. Regan never answered the question. For at that moment her young son Tommie burst through the door, his necktie dangling from his collar. "Hey, Ma, tie this, will ya?" He caught sight of Julie. "Oh, hi," he said. "Doris went a'ready. Mr. Hampton and Bets picked her up in their car."

And not me. Not me ever any more. Julie's last hope burst into a thousand piercing fragments and she trembled with the pain of it. For this could be no accident. This they had planned, and even the sight of her as she rounded the bend had not softened their intent.

Mrs. Regan snatched at the ends of Tommie's tie and yanked them savagely.

"Hey, ouch!" he protested, but Julie did not hear. More vividly than when it had pulled out from the curb, she saw the Hamptons' car driving off without her and now, at last, anger mingled with her hurt.

So! They thought she was not good enough for them, just because of the color of her skin. Well, she'd show them! She'd show Doris and Bets and everyone that she was as good as anyone else!

Julie turned quickly away from the Regans so they would not see her tears. Then she threw back her head, gripped her pocketbook hard and started off toward school alone.

2

JULIE STOOD A LITTLE BEHIND THE MOB GATHERED AROUND the bulletin board. It was one thing to say you were as good as anyone else but quite another to push in where you might not be wanted. She had to see that board to find out where her home room would be, but she could wait.

A girl backing away from the board jostled against her, and Julie jumped, an apology on her lips. "Excuse me."

"Excuse *me*," said the jostler and Julie saw that her blue-gray eyes crinkled in a smile.

The girl went on talking. "Isn't this gruesome? I thought high school would be dignified." She laughed. "I practiced acting like a lady all summer and now look." Her hand swept out in a broad gesture that covered the group fighting its way to the bulletin board and the boys and girls who talked too loudly as they clattered along the corridor behind them.

"It isn't the way I thought it would be either." Julie spoke without bitterness, not thinking of Bets and Doris but only of the noise and confusion.

"Well, no use to hang around here all day. 'Bye." The girl started to walk away and it was as if the sun had gone under the clouds until she turned back with a grin. "See you," she said and hurried off.

Julie watched the light-brown curls as they disappeared into the crowd, and a little smile formed on her lips. Then she began to work her way to the bulletin board, not pushing, not shoving, but definitely moving forward.

She found her home-room number, found the room too. Hesitant, self-conscious, she crossed the threshold. And there, over by the window, was Doris her red hair fiery in the sunlight, a sparkle and glint at her waist—the studded belt Julie had given her on her last birthday.

They met at close range when they left the room. Doris said, "Hi," with a nervous giggle.

"Hello, Doris." Julie was cautious.

"Look." Doris' eyes darted all around Julie's face. "I didn't call you because Mr. Hampton offered to drive me to school. It wasn't my car, so I couldn't very well invite you. Could I?"

"No." There was nothing else to say.

"The trouble is—you see, he's driving us tomorrow too. It's such a long walk, I mean, you wouldn't want me to give up a chance for a ride, would you?"

"Of course not." The lie fell from Julie's lips with amazing ease.

"So. Okay, then." Doris smiled weakly and scuttled into the crowd.

Julie moved more slowly, moved through the morning in a daze of hubbub and rush and jumbled impressions. There were new faces and old, pink cheeks and summer tans, and now and then, though rarely, a boy or girl with skin as brown as her own. There were smiles and indifference, voices that pierced the air around her and some that paused to speak kindly. An older girl would stop to say, "You seem to be having trouble. May I help you find your way?"

At lunchtime, not quite able to face the cafeteria alone, Julie wandered into the yard. The sun blinded her so that when she stepped into the shade of an oak, she did not see the girl who sat half hidden by its trunk. It was the movement that caught her eye. A dark head leaned around to look at her, and a face, much lighter than her own but still not white, smiled.

"Hello," said the girl.

"Oh, excuse me. I didn't know there was anyone here." Julie started to back away.

"That's all right. Sit down." The girl patted the ground at her side. "You bring your lunch?"

"No, I didn't." Julie lowered herself to the grass.

"Have some of mine."

"Oh, no. Thank you." Julie pushed at the paper bag that had been thrust toward her.

"Come on."

"Well—all right." This time Julie reached into the bag and pulled out a sandwich.

"Are you a freshman?" the girl wanted to know.

Julie had bitten into the sandwich, and dry peanut butter stuck to her teeth and the roof of her mouth so that all she could say was, "Um-hm."

"Well, it's all right to bring your lunch. I'm a freshman too, but my sister told me. She graduated two years ago. You can eat it in the cafeteria if you want to, but it was such a nice day I thought I'd come out here."

"It's fun," Julie said. "Tomorrow I'll bring mine."

"That'll be nice. What's your name, anyway? Mine's Marilyn Hall."

"Julie. Julie Brownell."

"Really? That's our doctor's name. Brownell, I mean."

"He's my father."

"No kidding!"

Both girls smiled, pleased at knowing someone in common.

As they ate their lunch, other boys and girls began to drift out through the doors. Soon the yard was gay with bright dresses and flashy shirts, with laughter and shouts and squeals of reunion.

"Looks pretty, doesn't it?" Marilyn said. "All those colors on the green grass."

"Mm."

"Say! There's David Ross. And Rickie Sheridan." Marilyn leaped up and smoothed her skirt over her hips. "Dave!" she called. "Hi!"

In the farthest shade of the tree, two boys stopped but

came no nearer. Two hands rose in a quick salute, one white, the other brown.

The Negro was apparently David Ross, for he was the one who responded to Marilyn's call. "Hey! Who let you in here?"

"Aw, don't listen to him." The white boy shoved at Dave, pushing him off balance. "They let you in, didn't they?"

"Rickie! Take it easy, will ya?" Dave's fist shot out and thumped against Rickie's ribs. He grinned at Marilyn and pointed at his friend with staccato movements of his thumb. "Wise guy."

"Wise guy, yourself." Rickie laid his hand on Dave's shoulder. "You got any more insults to hand out or shall we shove?"

"Sociable character, isn't he?" Dave jerked his head sideways at Rickie. "Okay. Let's go." He waved at Marilyn. Rickie waved, too, and the boys moved on.

Marilyn rubbed one hand over her hair and down the back of her neck. "Dave doesn't care much about girls," she said softly, "but if he ever does, I declare I'm going to be around."

Julie glanced up at Marilyn, feeling suddenly strange. She and Bets and Doris had talked about boys but never with such confidence. She looked again at the two fellows as they walked off together, one with his hand on the shoulder of the other, and the sight of the boy who had been able to keep his white friend sharpened her sense of loss and desolation.

"Julie!" Marilyn whirled toward her. "I never introduced you. I'm sorry! Why didn't you kick me or something?"

"That's all right." Warmed by Marilyn's concern, Julie rose to stand beside her.

A bell clanged. The leisurely scene in the school yard turned to one of bustle as the bright colors converged toward the doorways. Julie and Marilyn, both at once, bent to pick up their lunch papers. Their heads cracked together, nearly knocking them down, and they were off into gales of laughter.

Julie did not meet Bets until the end of the afternoon. Tired and a little hungry, she hurried along toward the door, glad to escape at last. But on the steps outside stood Bets, pretty in a crisp blue dress, her blond hair newly styled in a sleek, short bob. Though she was talking to a strange girl, Julie stopped involuntarily and before she could start on, Bets hailed her.

"Hi, Julie."

Unlike Doris, she sounded perfectly natural and Julie, daring to hope, let her words spill out too fast. "Hi, Bets. How're you? Did you have a good time at your grand—"

Bets cut her off. "This is Beverly Blake. Julie Brownell." She smiled at her new friend. "Way I happen to know Julie, we were in the same class in grade school."

Julie's raw wound burst wide open. Then, like the sting of iodine, rage flooded over it, pushing up through her chest and into her throat. Beverly's "Hello, Julie," was cordial, but Julie could only choke out a hostile-sounding, "Hello." She ran down the steps and along the walk, blind and deaf to every sight and sound.

At the gate a big fellow pulled away from the crowd and stepped toward her. "Julie! What's the matter?"

"George!" She had never been so glad to see anyone.

"Has someone been bothering you?" George's eyes scanned the steps behind her back. Julie turned to follow his gaze and saw that Bets was still there. For a second she wanted to tell. George would smash Bets' mouth so that it could never again explain her away. But she shook her head.

"No one's been bothering me."

George stared at her hard and shrugged. "I'll find out," he threatened. "Come on, Julie. I'll walk you home."

He left her at the bottom of her steps. Wearily she began the long climb, but in sight of her house she stopped. Mother would be there, anxious to hear about all that had happened, ready with words of sympathy. Julie did not want any sympathy, especially from the mother who had done so little to prepare her for this day. But how could Mother have told her? How could anyone talk about a hurt that went so deep?

Nor can I, Julie thought, and with a new agility her mind began to pick bright moments from the long hours just past. That nice girl at the bulletin board. Marilyn Hall who had shared her lunch. The older girls who had stopped to direct her, and George, who had seen her all the way home.

Julie took a breath so deep it made her shudder. Until yesterday she had run to her folks with every childish confidence, but now she started on, ready with a censored version of her day.

3

TOWARD THE END OF THE WEEK, JULIE STOOD AGAIN BEFORE the bulletin board and saw one notice which, for her, stood out above all the rest:

GLEE CLUB
Watch for notice of tryouts.
All freshmen invited.

She clasped her books more tightly to her chest. The high school glee club! All her life she had dreamed of becoming a singer; for years she had looked forward to being a part of this club. But now? Did they mean all freshmen? Or had Doris and Bets acted with some foreknowledge that from here on the white world would shut her out?

With the ache of Doris and Bets still a weight in her chest, with the coveted glee club membership strong in her heart, Julie watched and waited. But how could she tell? Girls like Anna Jensen, the one who had jostled against her on that first day, were always cordial and friendly. Yet why did they never include her in their plans?

Of course she was not alone. In the big freshman class there were four or five girls of her own race with whom she could make friends and eat her lunch. Especially there was Marilyn Hall, so little and pretty, with hair that fell around her neck. Marilyn, with her quick laughter and ready smile; with her everlasting sketch pad.

"Sit still, Julie. How can I get your profile if you keep looking at me?"

"Hey, Julie, let's walk along the river. I want to sketch some water and trees and stuff."

"Why'n't you come to my house, Marilyn? You can see all that from there."

"I know. But I didn't like to ask."

"You're silly."

"And you're lucky." Marilyn spoke without envy. "From the windows of our apartment there's not a tree in sight."

I'm lucky to have you for a friend, Julie thought, as she sat on the steps of her porch and watched Marilyn at work. They chatted until the sun was low in the sky and Marilyn began to gather her things. She spoke without looking up.

"I suppose you think it's funny I haven't invited you to my place."

"It doesn't matter." But Julie had thought it strange. She and Doris and Bets had been in and out of each other's houses nearly every day.

"I don't know if you'd like it," Marilyn explained. "You

see, we have only four rooms and there are eight of us counting my father and mother. It's kind of crowded."

"I like big families," Julie assured her. "Dor—that is, I used to have a friend with a batch of brothers and sisters and we had more fun at her house than anywhere else."

"Well, if you're sure you won't mind the mob." Marilyn stood up. "Come Saturday, Julie. My sister Lorraine will be home then, and she's just dying to meet you."

"Isn't that the sister who's finished school?"

"The only one I have. The others are all boys."

Julie wondered why an older girl would want to meet her, but it was flattering and when Saturday came she dressed with special care. She decided on her dark plaid skirt with a white blouse and rust-colored cardigan and fussed for a long time with the stubborn friz of her hair.

It was a blustery day. As Julie walked between the rows of dismal apartments on Marilyn's street, papers swirled around her legs and dirt blew against her face. Just when she reached the Halls' address, a speck of dust lodged in her eye and instantly tears began to stream down her cheek. What a way to make an impression! She opened the door and stumbled up the dark stairway, hardly able to see a thing.

Marilyn answered her knock. "Julie! What's happened to you?"

"Something in my eye." Julie sniffed, for by this time her nose was running too.

"Well, come in."

As Julie stepped through the door, her good eye saw a tall girl walking toward her and she nearly gasped. For if Marilyn was pretty, this girl was beautiful; if Marilyn was light-skinned, this girl was almost white; and her hair, pulled into a low bun, was practically straight. When she spoke her voice was soft and clear as a tinkling bell.

"You poor thing!" She took Julie's arm and led her to a chair. "We'll fix you, though. Marilyn, would you please get a clean handkerchief from my drawer?"

"Maybe it will wash out." Julie felt awkward.

"And maybe not. By the way, I'm Lorraine."

"I thought so. I'm Julie."

Lorraine removed the speck gently and with deftness. "There now." She handed Julie the handkerchief. "Use this. Yours must be all soppy."

Julie's eyes still blinked but now she could see the room, neat and clean, though cluttered with too much furniture. Marilyn plopped down on one of the iron cots and Lorraine pulled up a straight-backed chair next to Julie.

"It's so nice to have you here," she said. "We think a great deal of your father. Tell us about you."

"There's nothing to tell." Julie cocked her head in a gesture of self-consciousness.

"There is so!" Marilyn said. "Julie can play the piano like an angel."

"I can't! Anyway, angels don't play pianos. They play harps."

How had she ever thought to say that? It made them all laugh, and Julie, more at ease, turned to Lorraine. "What do you like to do?"

Marilyn took over again. "Lorraine's smart. She made the Honor Society at school and she takes night courses at New York University."

"Stop it, Marilyn." Lorraine smiled and waved a hand at her sister. "Anyone can take courses."

Marilyn did not stop. "She has a good job too."

Lorraine's smile faded abruptly and an expression of discontent spread across her face. "Don't say that! It isn't true. I have a job. Period."

"Well, you have a job and that's more than some people." Lorraine had withdrawn into herself and Marilyn looked troubled. "Oh, I wish you had let the boys stay in! We never would have started talking about this."

Lorraine snapped out of her mood with a chuckle of amusement. "You're right about that. We wouldn't have been able to talk at all. They were crazy to see you, Julie, but when they're here it's like victory day on a football field."

"Mother's not home either," Marilyn said. "She's working, and Dad . . ."

Lorraine interrupted. "Julie doesn't want to hear our whole family history. Suppose I get us some refreshments." She left the room, her high heels clacking on the bare floor.

"She's adorable!" Julie said.

"Thanks." Marilyn pulled her feet up under her. "I like her, too, only . . ."

"Only what?"

"She's always—she can't ever relax."

Then I'll never relax either, Julie resolved. For to her the beautiful soft-voiced Lorraine exemplified perfection.

September passed and October began to color the trees, tentatively at first and then in an unrestrained splash of brilliance. The first time Marilyn saw it from Julie's hillside house, she was breathless. "Oh-h-h!" was all she said.

"Well, get busy." Julie picked up the sketch pad that had dropped from Marilyn's hand.

"I'd need oils for this," Marilyn said. "But maybe next year."

"Won't your folks give you any?"

"Mercy, no!" Marilyn's laughter rang. "What do you think they'd use for money?"

"Oh." Julie wished she had been more thoughtful, and felt a little guilty about her piles of sheet music and shelves of recordings. "Stay for dinner," she said impulsively.

"I'd like to." Marilyn ruffled her pad. "Only don't you have to ask your mother?"

"No. I can have company whenever I want."

Marilyn considered her seriously for a moment, then

laughed again. "I must say, there are advantages to being an only child."

There are disadvantages, too, Julie decided as she and Marilyn laughed and chattered their way through dinner. If she had a sister like Marilyn, always so cheerful and so much fun, maybe all the meals would be like this. Maybe she could throw off the burden of her parents' constant concern.

When they had finished their dessert, Dr. Brownell pushed back his chair. "Looks as if none of my patients will need me tonight. How about a little singing?"

Julie looked across the table at her guest. "I don't know, Daddy. Maybe Marilyn doesn't like to sing."

"But I do!" Marilyn's lively eyes reflected the glow of the candles on the table.

Julie's mother was not a musician but sat as an appreciative audience while her father played and sang in accompaniment to the girls. Engrossed in the music, Julie did not notice when Marilyn stopped and withdrew to the davenport. It was not until the song was ended that she turned to her friend and found she was not at her side.

"Where's—oh, there you are. What's the matter, Marilyn? Want to stop?"

"Oh, no. That is, I don't want you to stop. Julie, you never told me you could sing. I mean, really sing."

"Well . . ." Julie, embarrassed but pleased, too, looked away from Marilyn and smiled at her father.

"But you didn't sign up for glee club," Marilyn said. "Didn't you see the notice? It was posted yesterday."

The smile stiffened on Julie's lips. She could not pull her eyes away from her father's questioning look, his anxious scrutiny. "Yes, I—saw it."

"Then why didn't you sign it, for lands' sake?" Marilyn was on her feet.

If only Daddy would not understand! If only Marilyn would! Caught between the two pressures, Julie flung out crossly, "Because I don't want to."

She saw Marilyn's baffled hurt, heard her mother's reproof. "Julie, dear!"

"I'm sorry, Marilyn." Julie held out her hand. "Let's go up to my room. I'll show you my new hat."

But Julie did not show Marilyn her new hat. She got as far as her closet door and stood there with her back to her friend. "Marilyn?"

"Yes?"

"Would you join the glee club?"

"That's different. I can't sing."

"But if you could?" Julie turned halfway around.

Marilyn took a long time to answer. She sat on the bed and stared at her fingers as they locked and unlocked in her lap. "I know what you mean, Julie. No, I guess I wouldn't."

"See?" Julie's tone was edged with triumph.

"I suppose it's the same for all of us," Marilyn said. "Sometimes they seem to want us and then suddenly they don't. Lorraine says we'll never get anywhere if we don't keep trying but I—I guess I just don't have the courage." Marilyn's rueful smile was a plea for understanding.

"Lorraine?" Julie forgot Marilyn. "Was she in any of the clubs at school?"

"Sure. She'd have a fit if she knew I wouldn't apply for sketch club, but I wouldn't, not for anything. I suppose she's right, only . . ." Marilyn laughed apologetically. "But I can't draw as well as you can sing. You're so terrific, they couldn't possibly turn you down."

"I don't know!" Julie could see the notice as clearly as if it were printed on the rug. All freshmen invited. That was the school policy, but there could be people stronger than regulations, and an air of unwelcome as hard to hurdle as a high fence. Lorraine had leaped the barrier, but Lorraine looked white. Julie dug her nails into the palms of her hands. Lorraine would have tried in any case.

In the morning Julie did not wait for Marilyn in front of the school but went directly into the building, straight to the bulletin board. She studied the list of those who had signed up for the tryouts and each name brought a picture to her mind. Anna Jensen with her light-brown curls. Louis Stevens with his red crew cut and freckles. Maureen Kelly with her Irish blue eyes.

There was a pencil dangling on a string beside the list. Julie picked it up, dropped it. Then quickly she picked it up again and added her name to the list.

On the day of the tryouts she was the first to arrive. She

sat down in the end seat of the front row of the music room and wished she were at the North Pole, the South Pole, anywhere but here. What would the others say when they saw her? Or what if she should get up there at the piano and be so scared that her voice would not come out at all?

Two girls came in, arm in arm. They smiled at Julie and sat in the same row, leaving a vacant seat between themselves and her. Two boys shuffled past her and fell noisily into chairs beside the girls. Rickie Sheridan went by but without that nice David Ross. More boys, more girls and always the vacant seat.

At the last minute Anna Jensen dashed breathlessly through the door. "Am I late? Where's Miss Williams? Oh, hello, Julie."

She teetered in front of the empty seat, waving and calling to her friends. Julie held her breath until, abruptly, Anna sat beside her.

"I'm scared stiff," she said to Julie. "You?"

"Yes, I am!" Julie was glad now for the fear that joined her to Anna.

Miss Williams appeared in the doorway and scurried past the piano, talking as fast as she walked. "Oh dear! Oh dear! I'm late. Couldn't help it. Couldn't help it." Even her smile was harried, and one wisp of gray hair had come loose from the bun in her neck and dribbled along her thin sallow cheek.

"Well, well, well," she said. "Isn't this lovely? All these

boys and girls. Of course we can't all be in the glee club, but we'll see. We'll see."

Feet shuffled on the floor. One or two people coughed. Anna let out her breath in a kind of giggle.

"Now," said Miss Williams. "Let's warm up our voices. We'll sing something together, something we all know. *America?*"

"We don't know that," quipped Rickie Sheridan from the second row.

But Miss Williams' arms were already sweeping up high over her head. "Rise, please."

Julie almost laughed when the music teacher sounded the note, a long tremulous, "Do-o-o." They started to sing, and Miss Williams led them, flinging her arms, body and head about like a bare tree as it sways in a storm.

At least I'm not going to be afraid of her, Julie thought. Just the same, when her turn came she walked to the piano on wobbly legs. Like the others, she sang up and down the scale; unlike the others, every note was firm and true. Like the others, she read a few lines of music; unlike the others, she did not hesitate and stumble. In the third test, a simple hymn, the difference was not only in herself but in the boys and girls behind her. The wriggling stopped; there were no more whispers and giggles.

When she finished, Miss Williams stared at her as if she were a freak. "An unusual voice. Very unusual." She picked up the slip with Julie's name on it, thrusting out her chin to read it through the bottom of her bifocals. "Julie

Brownell," she said and she put the slip on the left-hand pile on top of the piano.

"You made it. I'm sure you did," Anna whispered as Julie returned to her seat. "All the good ones were put on that pile."

"Where did she put yours?" Julie wished she had noticed.

"I don't know. I was too scared to look."

The next day when Julie and Marilyn went to check on the list of successful candidates, Anna was just turning away from the bulletin board.

"Congrats, Julie. You're in," she said.

"I am? What about you?"

"I made it too. Don't ask me how, but I did." As always, Anna grinned, then hurried off.

But Marilyn was there and she squeezed Julie's arm. "Isn't it exciting, Julie? Aren't you glad you tried out?"

"Oh, Marilyn, yes!" Only now with Anna out of sight did Julie fully realize that her ambition had been achieved. She was a member of the high school glee club! But what was in it for Marilyn, so happily beaming at her side? If only . . .

"Marilyn! Try for sketch club. It's really not so bad."

"I . . ." Marilyn's grip on her arm loosened, tightened again. "All right. I will."

"That's wonderful!" For a moment Julie felt as strong and mature as Lorraine, able to boost others by her own example. Then Bets and that Beverly Blake walked past, so engrossed in each other they did not see Julie at all. Both of them wore the red and white ribbons that meant they had been pledged to the Zeta Tau sorority. Would anything ever open that door to Julie or Marilyn or anyone like them?

4

JULIE WAS WAITING FOR HER FATHER INSIDE THE STREET
entrance of the Halls' apartment. Lorraine stood beside her,
hugging herself against the chill night air that seeped in
around the edges of the door.

"I don't really have a letter to mail," she said. "I just
wanted to talk to you and there's no privacy upstairs."

"To me?" Julie looked up expectantly.

"Yes. I haven't had a chance to thank you for getting
Marilyn to join the sketch club. She's so apt to just take
what comes. She's like . . ." Lorraine shook her head and
in the light of the dim overhead bulb, Julie saw her frown.

"Well, Marilyn loves to draw." Though she spoke Marilyn's name, Julie was not thinking about her, not then.
Lorraine knew! Lorraine approved!

"I don't know whether she has any talent, but she might
make something of it if she'll only try." Lorraine laid her
hand on Julie's shoulder. "I'd better not keep you. Your
father's probably here by now."

"I guess. Good night, Lorraine. And thanks." Julie ran
lightly out to the waiting car.

"I'm sorry, Daddy. Have you been here long?"

"Just got here. You had fun, didn't you, Julie?"

"Oh, yes!" Julie was too elated to mind that her father had probed her feelings again, for she had had a happy evening. Mrs. Hall was so cordial and motherly. If only Mr. Hall could get a job so she wouldn't have to go out as a cleaning woman! He was such fun with his teasing and jokes, and so were the noisy boys.

They had put Julie into a gay mood and on the way home she never stopped chattering about them and about tomorrow's big event, the first rehearsal of the glee club.

The first rehearsal! All the next day it formed a refrain in her mind and in her eagerness she arrived early. Someone was ahead of her, though, a girl at the piano with Miss Williams, singing the simple hymn of the tryout. Julie pressed against the wall, not wanting to disturb her.

Miss Williams was undecided. "I don't know what to say. I don't know. You do qualify, but the glee club is filled up."

"Please, Miss Williams. Please!" The girl's head turned slightly and Julie saw that it was Beverly Blake.

Miss Williams struck an absent-minded chord. "All right. I'll try you. Someone is sure to drop out."

"Oh, thank you!" Beverly whirled away from the piano and caught sight of Julie. "Hey!" She came toward the wall. "I'm in the glee club."

"Congratulations." Julie smiled.

Miss Williams twisted around to squint at her. "Oh," she said. "You're that voice."

Beverly clapped her hand over her mouth to cover an explosive giggle. "I'm sorry, Julie. Please don't think I was laughing at you, but it sounded so funny. As if you were some kind of spook with nothing but a voice."

"That's all right."

Beverly was always overly polite, as if Julie were a piece of delicate china. Today she was more chatty than usual as she explained why she had not been at the tryouts. "I had laryngitis and couldn't have made a frogs' chorus."

"It's nice you could have another chance." Julie was reserved, constrained by the memory of their first meeting.

"Here come some Zeta Taus." Beverly dashed off.

Julie, left alone, watched the others with quiet interest. These were the people with whom she would share her singing, the ones who might become her friends. Already Anna Jensen—but where was the girl?

Anna was late, as usual. By the time she came in Miss Williams had begun to group the different sections, and Julie was seated with the altos, far from Anna and what Anna, herself, called her high soprano squeak.

The rehearsal began, and Julie forgot everything else. This was what she had waited for, this blending of her voice with all those others; she was careful not to use its full power lest she spoil the choral effect of the whole. It was rough and blundering this first time, but she loved every minute. It seemed as if they had only begun when Miss Williams said, "That's all for today, boys and girls."

With the singing over, Julie was alone again. But each week she was a little more included. There was a gradually increasing chorus of "Hi, Julie" to greet her; talk which took her presence for granted even when it inadvertently shut her out.

"You going to Beverly's party?"

"Natch. Everyone is."

Well, she couldn't hope for parties, but maybe some day she would be invited to join one of the groups that hustled off for Cokes after rehearsals.

If only some of her own friends were in the club! The only other Negro was a senior boy, and he paid no attention to Julie or any other girl.

"I'd make him pay attention," Marilyn told her, but Julie was far too shy even to say hello.

At the fourth rehearsal Miss Williams picked her out to demonstrate a difficult passage. "Where's that voice? You!" she snapped, thrusting a bony finger at Julie.

Startled as she was, Julie managed to run through the passage without a quaver.

"Weren't you nervous?" Anna asked afterward. "I mean, in front of all those juniors and seniors."

"No, not really," Julie said. "I wonder if they minded, though. After all, I'm only a freshman."

Whether the upperclassmen objected or not, Julie's performance gave her a new standing among her classmates.

The next week several of them greeted her as The Voice, the nearest any of them had come to natural banter. And Beverly asked to sit beside her.

"I simply can't get that alto part, but if you're next to me, maybe I can follow you."

It was the best rehearsal so far—not yet good, but Julie's sensitive ear caught the improvement. It gave her a wonderful sense of satisfaction, like that of a builder who starts with nothing and watches his structure gradually take on form and substance.

Even when the rehearsal was over, she was still aglow with the excitement of the music. She turned to Beverly with eagerness and, for once, without restraint. Before she could say a word, the girl on her right leaned across in front of her.

"Say, Bev. How about a Coke? I'm about to die of thirst."

"Sure." With a mumbled, "Excuse me," Beverly squeezed past Julie as if she were not there at all.

The joy drained out, leaving Julie shaken. She watched Beverly and her friend as they pushed through the crowd arm in arm. Then she reached for her books and hurried across the room with her eyes on the door, as if she had not the time to speak to anyone on the way.

She would not give them another chance to snub her! At the following rehearsal she purposely arrived late and slipped into her place at the last minute. She meant to leave promptly, too, but Miss Williams stopped her.

"I heard Marian Anderson in New York last night. Beautiful voice. Beautiful."

"Yes, I know." Julie was no Marian Anderson, and she was embarrassed by Miss Williams' racial implication in choosing to tell only her. "I—we have some of her recordings."

"How nice!" Miss Williams' attention was suddenly diverted by someone who stood behind Julie. "Yes? What is it?" she asked impatiently.

"I'm in no hurry." It was Anna's pleasant voice.

Julie started to move away, but Anna signaled her to wait. It appeared she was going away for Thanksgiving and wanted to be excused from the next rehearsal in order to get an early start. This brought a long oration from Miss Williams so by the time Julie and Anna left the room was nearly empty.

"Thanks, Julie," Anna said as they walked along the corridor. "I didn't want to get murdered without someone there to pick up the pieces."

Julie chuckled. "Miss Williams wasn't exactly pleased, was she?"

They pushed through the heavy outside door into a raw gray afternoon. A bunch of girls was huddled on the steps, and one of them called to Anna.

"It's about time. Where you been?"

"Simmer down," Anna said cheerfully. She grinned at Julie. "We're going to The Hangout for Cokes. Want to come?"

Julie's eyes darted over the waiting group.

"Just make up your mind, that's all." A red-faced girl turned up the collar of her coat. "I'm frozen." There was no malice in her tone, nor any careful politeness. It was almost as if she were Marilyn or one of Julie's other cafeteria table mates.

"I'd love to come," Julie said.

She had a wonderful time. New to the group, feeling her way, she said little, but she enjoyed the chatter of the others and the giggling. When they parted at the corner, the girl who had sat beside her said, "Nice having you along, Julie. Do it again some time."

Julie flew home on winged feet. At last she was a club member in the true sense. Maybe it was not like the prestige of David Ross who, with his pal Rickie Sheridan, was making a name for himself in cross-country track. But it was a start, and nothing could take it away.

At home she found Aunt Helen in the living room with her mother, and she stopped in the doorway to say hello.

"Hello, Julie," Aunt Helen said. "I haven't seen you for a long time. How are things going at school?"

"Fine, thanks." Julie wriggled out of her coat and tried to think how to get away, for Aunt Helen would surely ask about her son George. "Look, why don't I fix you some tea?"

She did not want to talk about George, especially to Aunt Helen. She had not forgotten his kindness during those first few days, but his reputation was a constant source of embarrassment. How much worse it must be for his mother! Besides, though she would never high-hat him, the truth was Julie avoided him as much as she could.

The very next day George was back to lend a helping hand. In the morning Julie awoke to the sound of rain, and by the time she and Marilyn came out of school in the afternoon, it had become a bad storm. Torrents fell from the sky and blew in great sheets across the yard. Cars were lined up on both sides of the street, their horns tooting impatiently above the roar of the wind.

"Looks as if all the parents in town had come to collect their kids," Marilyn observed.

"Not ours, though," Julie said. "Daddy has office hours at this time of day."

"I suppose we might as well drown now as later." Marilyn pulled her thin coat across her chest. "Let's go."

The two girls sloshed down the steps and along the walk, their heads bent against the wind. Neither of them saw the battered car that had won the favored spot next to the gate until its door opened a crack and someone called, "Julie."

"It's your cousin. It's George."

"Step on it," George shouted. "I'm getting soaked."

"You'll take Marilyn, too, won't you?" Julie asked.

"Sure."

Marilyn slid in beside George and Julie climbed after her.

"George, you're something!" Marilyn's eyes shone. "How did you ever manage to park next to the gate?"

"Huh. I'm smart." George looked pleased as he began to maneuver the car out of its parking place.

"But how did you go home and get back so soon?" Julie wanted to know.

"Just left school early. No one can make me stay if I don't feel like it." Already George had the car on its way and was weaving in and out of traffic with little regard for his own or anyone else's fenders. Once he narrowly missed a Ford coming in the opposite direction, and Julie cried out, "George! Be careful!"

Marilyn giggled. "That was neat."

Despite George's efforts, it took a long time to get out of the congestion around the school, and many of the boys and girls who had had to walk had made faster progress. This annoyed him and he bore down hard on the gas pedal. The car spurted forward, then abruptly slowed.

"Who's that?" George nodded toward two girls on the opposite sidewalk.

Through the clear spot made by the windshield wiper, Julie recognized Bets' yellow raincoat and Doris' plaid. A nameless fear kept her silent but at the sound of the stopping car, the girls turned around and Marilyn quickly identified them. "It's Bets Hampton and Doris something-or-other. What's her last name anyway, Julie?"

George did not wait for an answer but again stepped on the gas. The car shot across the street and streaked past Doris and Bets, sending a shower of muddy water over their sodden head scarfs and dripping raincoats. Julie slapped her hands over her eyes, but she could feel Marilyn wriggling beside her, hear her laughter.

"Shall I do it again?" George asked.

"Ye-e-es," squealed Marilyn.

"Don't you dare!" Julie's voice shook with anger.

George whipped the car around for another attack. Julie saw Bets and Doris huddled together against the fence at the far side of the walk, but beyond the fence there was a sheer drop so they could not escape the second splashing nor the third. Her protests were useless as Marilyn bounced on her seat, egging George on with joyous shrieks.

It seemed a year before they headed for home. Julie sat in her corner, stiff and straight, too furious to say a word.

"You were mean, George, mean." Marilyn spoke in tones of praise. She laughed again. "Their faces! Did you see their faces?"

George's lips were set in tight lines, and he made no comment. Marilyn looked nervously from him to Julie. "Maybe we shouldn't have done it, but it's only mud, Julie. It'll wash off."

Julie could not answer, nor did George.

"Well, gee!" Marilyn sounded almost desperate. "Maybe Doris is all right, but that Bets! She's such a big snob."

Not until the car stopped at Julie's steps did George speak. "I told you I'd find out."

Julie's dam broke. "George Thompson, you're nothing but a big bully. I suppose you think you're a hero, splashing a couple of girls. Well, you're not, and after this you can just keep out of my way."

"Aw, Julie, come off it. A little water never killed anyone. You know I wouldn't hurt a girl."

"Not much!" Julie jumped out of the car. "Good-bye!" she said and slammed the door.

By the time she had climbed the long stairway, her anger had drained off, leaving only despair. Why had he done it? Why? He did not want anyone to hurt her, that's what he said, and now he had fixed it so no one would ever speak to her again. Just when she had begun to make a little progress.

Mrs. Brownell met her at the door. "Julie, you must be drenched. Run up and change your clothes and I'll make us some hot cocoa."

At the sight of her mother, Julie's anger flared up again. It was her fault that George had found out about Doris and Bets. She must have told Aunt Helen yesterday while they waited for their tea.

"Mother, did you . . . ?" But of course her mother would not have hurt her purposely. What else could she have done when left alone to answer Aunt Helen's questions? "Okay. I'll go and change."

The cocoa warmed her body but not the bleakness in her heart. She tried to hide her mood and managed to talk of other things until her father came in and sat on the davenport beside her. At his, "How are you, Julie?" she burst into unexpected tears, and the whole story came out in a rush.

"Oh, Julie, Julie." Mother's face was etched in lines that reflected her daughter's anguish.

Dr. Brownell shook his head. "Poor children."

Julie's cup clattered against her saucer. "What children?" Was Daddy sorry for Doris and Bets?

"It's such a vicious circle," her father said sadly. "Society hurts George, and George tries to hurt back. But it doesn't help, Julie. Hate never helps."

Julie took a sip of cocoa and, for the first time, asked herself whether she hated Doris and Bets.

Daddy rubbed his gentle doctor's hand over her hair. "There's no use in my trying to evade. This will make it harder for you because when one Negro does something malicious, it is blamed on the whole race. But please don't meet it with hate, Julie. You'll only hurt yourself."

Julie got up to put her empty cup on the tray. No, she did not hate Doris and Bets, but with this knowledge another broke into her mind, frightening in its implication.

"But I don't care what happened to Doris and Bets! I did at first, but now I don't care at all. I can't help feeling that it serves them right."

Doctor Brownell's worried face relaxed. "That's a pretty healthy reaction, Julie. Now they're out of your system, I think you'll feel more kindly toward everyone, more free to go ahead and make new friends. You'll try, won't you?"

New friends? But you could not count on friends, not for a minute. Look at the way Marilyn had acted today.

"I'll see, Daddy." Julie took his cup. Yesterday she had found new friends, and what would they think of her now? Maybe she wouldn't even go back to glee club.

That thought startled her so that she nearly dropped the cup and saucer. Give up singing? Never! Her voice, her pleasure in using it, these were the things she could rely on, the substance of the dream that would never change.

She whirled back toward the davenport. "Daddy!" she said. "Mother! All I want is to be a singer. Why don't I start my training right now?"

✖ 5 ✖

FOR THE FIRST TIME IN HER LIFE, JULIE'S FATHER PUT HIS foot down. Within reason, he had always let her do pretty much as she wished, but in the matter of a singing career, he was unyielding.

"I know it's what you've always wanted, but it's too arduous a life, Julie. You could struggle for years and in the end find only disappointment. There's so little room at the top."

"But I wouldn't mind the work," Julie argued. "I wouldn't even mind not making the top if I could be doing what I like best."

"It isn't only the work," Daddy explained. "You'd get a lot of hard knocks along the way and you're so sensitive. You do have the voice, but I honestly don't think you have the temperament."

The discussion went on and on, and as Julie faced the consequences of her cousin's rowdy act, her protests gradually weakened. At the next glee club rehearsal, Bev Blake moved from her now accustomed place at Julie's side; afterwards her friends of the week before went off without a glance in her direction.

It was hardest with Anna Jensen.

"I told them it couldn't be true, Julie. I know it was your cousin, but it must have been some other girl."

"I—I was in the car," Julie had to admit.

"Then why didn't you stop him, for heaven's sake?"

Anna, I tried. I did try. Why couldn't I tell you? Why did I have to be loyal to George? Haunted by Anna's disillusioned expression, Julie was ready to abandon the struggle to make friends at school; ready, almost, to give in to her father's verdict.

Marilyn was remorseful. "I never thought it would turn out this way! Only—Julie, when you're with boys, don't you ever—I mean, don't you act the way they want, whether you like it or not?"

"I don't know any boys," Julie said, but she accepted Marilyn's explanation.

She could not forgive George, though. A few nights later when she sat in the living room making out her Christmas list, she wrote his name, then crossed it out with savage strokes of her pencil. The violence of her gesture made her father look up from his book.

"Having trouble, Julie?"

"No." Julie bent over the desk and doodled on her pad. There would be no Doris or Bets on the list this year, and who would come up late Christmas afternoon to sing carols and share cold turkey sandwiches and cider?

Mother said, "I wish there were someone we could invite for Christmas dinner."

Julie looked at Mrs. Brownell, who was cutting crepe-paper strips for her Brownie Scouts' next craft project. Funny, she had never realized what it must mean to Mother to have her own sister withdraw from family celebrations. All because of that George, who would have no part of them.

"We should be able to think of someone," Daddy mused. "But most of our friends will be with their relatives."

George's folks would not leave him alone at Christmas but they would come if he would, Julie thought. Maybe I could persuade him. But I won't. Not ever.

"I'll get some scissors and help you with those strips," she said. She sounded almost contrite.

She went upstairs for the scissors and when she returned, her father had had an idea. "We thought we could ask the Halls for our carol-singing party."

"All of them?" Julie stopped halfway across the room. That would mean Lorraine!

"Of course, all of them," Mother said. "It will be fun to have some young children around."

The Halls accepted the invitation, and Marilyn reported that Lorraine was giving the boys a course of manners such as they had never had.

"Why?" Julie asked. "My folks understand kids."

"You don't know my sister," Marilyn groaned. "She has to have everything just right."

Then our party will be just right, Julie resolved. If she

should get George to come to dinner, he would surely stay over and that would spoil everything.

Enwrapped in preparations for the coming holidays, the girls at school forgot about George. As their hostility lessened and disappeared, Julie found her tremulous eagerness returning. That feeling of being part of the school when the glee club sang at the closing assembly, that involuntary thrust of pleasure at Anna's offhand suggestion that they get together during vacation, weren't they worth striving for?

On Christmas Sunday, Julie and her mother went to church. They had fallen out of the habit of regular attendance because Dr. Brownell usually needed the car for calls, and it was a long bus trip. Packed into a pew, with the smell of pine decorations in the air and the strains of *Jesu Bambino* wheezing out of the old organ, Julie wondered why. There was a warmth here, a unity, which she did not find in any other place. And David Ross was in the pew across the aisle. Maybe if she came more often—but this was no time to think about boys.

After the service Julie reached the aisle just as David stepped from the pew on the opposite side. She managed a smile and a "Hello," and David said, "Hi, Julie."

He knew her name! Julie tried to think of something to say, but though they moved up the aisle side by side, no words would come. There was a little girl with David and she leaned around to gape at Julie, tugging at his sleeve.

"Oh, excuse me," David said. "Julie, this is my sister Penny."

"Hello, Penny." Julie was more at ease with children. "Are you all ready for Christmas?"

"Yes, ma'am!" The little girl spoke with such emphasis it made Julie want to laugh, and for a second David's eyes met hers in a smile, but she was overcome with shyness and looked away. Before she could recover, an elderly lady intercepted her.

"You don't know me, my dear, but I can't miss a chance to speak to that nice doctor's daughter."

Julie politely extended her hand, and her chance with David was gone.

She had lost her mother in the crowd but found her outside with Aunt Helen and Uncle Bill, who were waiting to drive them home. It made Julie uncomfortable, that drive, for it was a reminder of a job left undone. And it's going to stay undone, she promised herself, but it nagged at her all that day and the next until she was driven to put on her coat and start for George's house.

Maybe he won't be home, she hoped, but he was and alone, too, for Aunt Helen was helping Uncle Bill with the last-minute rush at his store. Julie plunged into the purpose of her visit the minute he had let her in.

"George, please come for Christmas dinner. You always used to, and it was so much fun."

"Christmas!" George turned away. "Lot of sentimental hooey."

Julie stared at his profile, floored by his attitude. "Well —George, please. Even if that's the way you feel, think what it would mean to our mothers."

"Our mothers!" George wheeled back, glaring. "What do we owe them?"

"George!" Julie's horror was tinged with a sudden awareness that she had sometimes come very near to that same thought. She covered her shame with anger. "Oh, you! You're an old—a—a Scrooge!"

"And you're a sucker," George retorted. "Bowing and scraping all over that school."

"I do not bow and scrape. I only—I only try to make friends." A sob escaped from Julie's throat, and the sound of it softened George.

"Oh, all right. I'll come this once. But if anyone makes any fuss about it, I'll walk right out. See?"

"They won't. I won't let them," Julie promised, but he had upset her and she felt uncertain. Maybe she had not done the right thing after all, for George in one of his sullen moods could ruin the day for everyone.

"Now what's wrong?" George growled. "I said I'd come, didn't I?"

"Nothing." Julie smiled to reassure him.

"Take your coat off, then. I'll see if there's anything to eat."

Not knowing how to get away, Julie followed him into the kitchen. When they found the cookie jar empty, she remembered the snacks of their childhood and said,

"I know. Let's make peanut butter and jelly sandwiches."

"Okay," George agreed, and Julie, with her lifelong familiarity with the Thompson kitchen, easily found the supplies and made the sandwiches while George poured Cokes. They both relaxed and were soon reminiscing like a couple of old cronies, with a remember this and a remember that sending them into rollicking laughter.

"That was fun," she told George when she left, and as she started home it crossed her mind that she had had somewhat the same sense of belonging she had noticed at church. But she wanted to belong at school, too, and now her cousin's accusations came back to trouble her. Did she really bow and scrape? Was it so awful to want acceptance beyond the little group with whom she ate lunch every day? And that about her mother. Why, she couldn't have resented her own mother! That wouldn't have been loyal even, and yet . . . She hurried her steps, eager to make restitution, glad she could offer Mother her sister for Christmas day.

When Mrs. Brownell heard the news, she was excited as a child. "It'll be like old times," she kept saying and it was a while before she came down to earth and bustled off to the phone to order a bigger turkey.

It certainly started like old times, for on Christmas Eve, Dr. Brownell was called from trimming the tree to attend a child who had had an overdose of candy or excitement.

"Mother! Why did you marry a doctor?" Julie teased.

"Because I loved him."

Sarah Lou bent to pick up an ornament. "You wait till you fall in love, Julie. You won't pay no heed to whether he's a doctor or what."

Julie grinned but her face felt warm. Why did Sarah Lou's remark make her think of David Ross?

Christmas morning held more than the usual anticipation, for Julie's expectancy, though heightened by the prospect of the party, was combined with uneasiness about George. Would he surely come? And how would he act?

For a while she was diverted by her gifts, the soft white sweater, the full skirt and crinoline, the gold charm bracelet, the pale-blue skating suit. Later when Mother had gone to help Sarah Lou, she occupied herself with last-minute dusting. But at the sound of footsteps on the porch she tensed, the dust cloth tight in her hand, while her father went to the door. "Make them come. Make them come," she whispered, but she did not dare look till she heard their voices. The Thompsons were here!

The dinner went off splendidly. George was quiet but not unpleasant, and it was not until they had started to nibble nuts that he became restless. By then Julie was fidgety, too, for at this rate they would not be ready for their company. She kept stealing glances at her watch, and finally asked her mother if she might clear the table.

"Of course, dear." Mrs. Brownell turned to Aunt Helen. "We're having a few people in to sing carols. You'll stay, won't you?"

"Oh, I don't know." Aunt Helen looked at her son.

"You stay. I gotta push off." George shoved his chair away from the table.

"Maybe we'd all better go," Aunt Helen said. "Soon as we've helped clean up."

"No, no. You stay. I gotta see some fellows." George was already standing up, thanking Mrs. Brownell for the dinner, saying, "S'long," in a way that left his folks no choice but to let him go without them.

Julie followed him into the hall. The wind was howling around the house, and through the living-room window beyond, she could see the gray clouds of the winter twilight in cold contrast to the brightly lighted tree. It seemed sort of sad for anyone to go out into such bleakness alone and on Christmas day. Without planning to, she touched her cousin's arm. "You'd better stay."

"Uh-uh. Not me. I don't go for parties."

"Marilyn Hall will be here."

"She will?" A flicker of interest showed in his eyes, but he turned to open the door of the coat closet. "Ah, she's just a kid."

"She likes you, though," Julie said.

"Yeah? She tell you that?"

"I just know it." Not used to dissembling, Julie quavered a little. Marilyn did like George, but so did she like anyone who was a fellow.

George said, "Hm. I suppose I could stick around. For a while, anyway."

"Good." Julie pushed him toward the living room. "You sit down while I clear the table."

At about five o'clock, the Halls literally blew in. The light-skinned boys had ruddy cheeks and red noses, and Lorraine's usually smooth hair had been tossed into wisps. Julie offered to take them upstairs, but Mr. and Mrs. Hall said they had climbed all the steps they could. The boys gravitated to the tree and Marilyn to George, so that only Lorraine followed Julie to her room. She stood on the threshold looking around and drew a deep breath. "It's lovely."

"What is?" Julie wanted to know.

"This room. This whole house." Lorraine moved across to the window and stood there with her beautiful profile and dark hair outlined against the white curtains. "Some day I'll have a home like this." She spoke with such solemnity that Julie felt awed, as if she were witnessing a dedicated moment.

Then, in one of her quick changes of mood, Lorraine turned around, laughing. "Listen to me! You'd think I didn't come up here to comb my hair."

At last they were all gathered around the piano and this, for Julie, was a highlight of the day. As they sang the old hymns and carols, *God Rest Ye Merry Gentlemen, Deck the Halls, Adeste Fideles*, she found, to her delight, that Mr. Hall had a deep, rich voice. Gradually, without particular plan, she moved closer to him, and their tones blended into a kind of duet, with the others singing an accompaniment. As always when she sang, she was lifted out of herself and had no thought except for the music.

They had been at it for some time when Dr. Brownell began to play *Oh, Holy Night*. As if by common consent, the others were silent, listening to Julie and Mr. Hall. But the boys had grown restless. Mild boxing matches were going on between them and when the chorus started, the ten-year-old fell on his knees as the words exhorted. The others followed his example with loud thuds and giggles.

"Who's hungry?" Dr. Brownell asked as the last chord died away.

"Me! Me! Me!" the boys shouted.

"All right. Just one more song," he said. "*Silent Night*. How would you boys like to have a quartet?"

"Who, us?" The oldest one looked pleased.

Dr. Brownell nodded. "Everyone else hum."

"Be serious now," Lorraine admonished, and they were. Julie, humming softly, watched their earnest faces, listened to their high clear voices, and tears came to her eyes.

They were earnest about eating, too. Sarah Lou made more and more sandwiches and the turkey, which only that morning had looked as if it would last forever, completely disappeared. Dishes of cranberry sauce were scraped clean, cider jugs emptied. Lorraine was embarrassed by their appetites and their mother worried lest they become sick.

"If they do there's a good doctor handy," Marilyn said,

and George laughed as if she had made a big joke. He had been on his best behavior all evening.

There were so many Halls that it took both Dr. Brownell and Uncle Bill to drive them home. When Julie and her mother had seen the last one out the door, Mrs. Brownell slipped her arm around her daughter's waist and together they went back to the living room.

"Have a good Christmas?" Mother asked.

"Wonderful! I love the Halls, don't you?"

"They're a nice family," Mother agreed.

Gently Julie pulled away from her mother and sat down on the piano bench with her back to the keyboard. They're nice and they're my friends, she thought. And George, if he always acted as he had today, and the people at church. Why do I bother with all those others?

She reached around to the piano and strummed the melody of *Silent Night*. It could always be like this, couldn't it? No, it could not. As long as she went to school, she could not be content until she was as much a part of that group as any other. And now, added to this longing was her father's challenge. If she should withdraw, he would never believe she could take the knocks along the way.

Julie swung around to the piano and struck the opening chords of *Finlandia*. Christmas was over.

6

JULIE EASED HER BOOKS ONTO THE RECEIVING DESK AND smiled at the elderly librarian.

"That was quite a load." The librarian returned her smile before she bent her head to examine the books. "My," she said pleasantly. "You must be interested in music."

"I am," Julie told her. "I'm going to be a singer."

"Oh." The librarian's face went blank; her voice turned vague. "That's nice."

A frown creased Julie's forehead as she walked away. Why did people look at her so strangely when she told them she meant to be a singer? First Miss Williams and now that librarian. Did they think it was hopeless for a girl like her, or did they share Mother's old-fashioned belief that people in the entertainment world were not quite nice?

Well, it didn't matter. It couldn't matter. Last night she had won a big concession from Daddy. In the few weeks since Christmas, having read every book the library had to offer on singing and singers, she had learned that it is not usually advisable for a girl to start voice training until the age of sixteen. And Daddy had promised to reconsider it at that time.

A year and a half seemed ages to wait, but it was not so long when considered in terms of overcoming her susceptibility to hurt, and this Julie knew she must do if she were to gain a favorable decision from Daddy. And so, after the next glee club meeting, she deliberately sought out the girls who had first offered and then withdrawn their friendship.

"Hey, Anna. You all going for Cokes?"

"Sure," Anna said. "We always do. How come you never came with us again?"

Because I wasn't invited, Julie could have told her, but later, sipping her Coke, she realized she had not needed an invitation. Anna's friends seemed to take her presence for granted, and they asked her if she didn't want to go skating the next day.

"Mm, yes!" Julie said. "I got a new skating suit for Christmas."

"What'd you do with it? Put it in moth balls?" someone asked. "The ice has been good for a week."

Afterward, Julie could only be sorry she had missed that first week, for there at the pond no lines were drawn. Boys and girls, freshmen, sophomores, juniors and seniors mingled to crack the whip, to race or to try fancy steps. The only flaw for Julie was David Ross, who never so much as noticed her presence. Of course she could hardly expect attention from the freshman wonder of the basketball court. Still, he had spoken to her that time in church, and she could not help hoping he would skate with her just once, as Louis Stevens had with Anna.

Not that Anna was satisfied. "I muffed it, Julie. What's the matter with me, anyway? I can talk to fellows around school, but the minute one of them really looks at me, I can't open my mouth. Do you ever get that way?"

"All the time!"

The two girls smiled at each other in wordless acknowledgment of this new bond between them.

If only Marilyn would come skating! She tried it once, but Lorraine's old skates fitted her poorly, and though Julie helped her most of the afternoon, she could not control the wobble of her ankles nor get the knack of it at all. On her fifth or sixth tumble, she sat back on the ice, her arms folded across her chest, and laughed at her own awkwardness.

"I give up," she said, and she never came again.

Nor could Julie interest the other girls with whom she always ate lunch. It was almost as if they preferred to isolate themselves from the rest of the class. Of the five, only Marilyn had joined a club; only Elise Atkins ever turned up at the pond.

So it was the glee club bunch with whom Julie went skating, and when the ice thawed, they continued to include her in their doings. She came to feel more and more as if she were one of them, yet there were times when she was not.

Again she tried to draw Marilyn into this crowd.

"Come for a walk with us tomorrow, Marilyn. We're going across the river."

"I can't." Marilyn looked up from her sketch pad. "Julie, will you please stay in one position!"

Julie moved back to rest one shoulder against the wall of the living room where, draped in a toga of window curtains, she was posing as a Roman. "Why can't you?"

"I don't know those girls very well." Marilyn squinted at Julie and added a few lines to her drawing.

"But they like you. Anna's always asking me to bring you along."

"She is?" Marilyn went on with her work. "Ya, but that's now. Later she might change her mind."

"Not Anna," Julie assured her.

But Marilyn only said, "I'm finished," and brought the sketch for Julie's inspection. "How do you like it?"

"It's—fine." Julie tried to hide her doubts. It did look something like the pictures in her Latin book, but not at all like herself.

"Do you really think it's good?" Marilyn looked at the picture critically. "Julie, wouldn't it be exciting if I turned out to be an artist? A really famous one, I mean. Marilyn Hall, the great painter." She strutted across the room, one hand on her hip, more like a Hollywood starlet than a feminine Michelangelo.

Julie rubbed her hands over the goose pimples on her

bare arms. "All I can say is, I hope I won't have to be the famous artist's model. I'm frozen."

Winter melted into spring and each week Julie became further absorbed into the activities that stemmed from school. Let Marilyn withdraw. That would not be Lorraine's way, nor could it be Julie's.

It was not always easy. Not after the glee club concert when a parent invited everyone else in her crowd for ice cream at The Hangout. Not the many times when she had to live down the embarrassment of George. It was worst the day he fought an Italian boy and hurt him badly.

Up at the Halls' that night, Marilyn defended him. "But the other fellow was picking on a little kid."

"I know, but why does he always have to fight?" Julie complained.

"We all have to fight in a way, just to hold our own," Lorraine said. "Don't let this throw you, Julie."

"I won't," Julie promised, and again she rode out the storm of disapproval.

In April, less than three weeks before the school orchestra was to give its concert, the piano accompanist broke her wrist. A call went out for a substitute, but none could be found.

"Why don't you do it, Julie?" Marilyn asked.

"I can't play. Not that well." They were changing for gym, and Julie bent to step into her uniform.

"Can you play at all?" Anna's voice was muffled by the sweater she was pulling over her head.

"A little," Julie admitted.

"For goodness' sake, let them know, then," Anna said. "They're so desperate they'll want you even if you stink."

Behind Anna, Beverly Blake froze, one sneaker grasped tightly in her hand. "Anna Jensen, what a thing to say! Julie doesn't stink at all."

"That's what you think." Anna grinned and flicked her sweater against Julie's face. Laughing, Julie snatched the sweater and tossed it onto the top of a locker, out of reach.

"See?" Anna unzipped her skirt and smirked at Beverly. "No, but seriously, Julie. If you can play, you ought to let them know."

Should she? To play in public might make her look like a dope, for she was not an expert pianist. Surely Daddy could not call this sensitivity. But what about the boys and girls in the orchestra? How would she have felt if something had happened at the last minute to spoil the glee club concert? Without telling anyone, she went to Mr. Feldman, the orchestra director, and offered her services.

"You're the answer to a prayer," he said. "Let's hear you play."

Julie ran through a Chopin waltz.

"Hm, nice." Mr. Feldman put a piece of music on the piano rack. The "Triumphal March" from *Aïda*. "Try this."

Opera! Julie could not find her handkerchief, so she

wiped her perspiring hands on her skirt. Still they slipped and slithered over the keys as she stumbled through the first two lines.

"That's enough," Mr. Feldman said.

Julie glanced up at him, then dropped her eyes. "Sounded more like a funeral march," she murmured.

"Needs practice," Mr. Feldman agreed. He picked up a pile of music from the top of the piano. "Think you can learn all this in two and a half weeks?"

"I—I . . ." She couldn't back out now. "I'll try."

Mr. Feldman handed her the music and patted her shoulder. "Don't worry about it. If I know my orchestra, there'll be more than one mistake."

Julie worked as she never had before. On the days when there were no rehearsals, she went directly home from school and practiced all afternoon. On week ends, some of the members of the orchestra came to her house to practice with her. Engrossed in the job, she never realized that she was making new friends.

Her parents were worried that she'd wear herself out, but Julie only smiled and said she wasn't tired at all. "I told you I'd never mind hard work if it was music," she reminded them.

Despite her effort, she had not achieved perfection by the night of the concert, and she took her place at the piano, weak with fright. Mr. Feldman stepped to the podium. He smiled once at the group before him and raised his baton.

Watch that baton, Julie told herself. Keep one eye on the music. Count the beats. Don't come in too soon. These thoughts crowded out her fear, and before she knew it, intermission had come. She had made mistakes, but so had some of the others, and while she could never be happy about flaws in music, it was fun to join the general bemoaning of errors and the hopes that the audience had not noticed.

The second half of the program went even more quickly than the first. Julie could hardly believe it when she heard the last applause and saw Mr. Feldman make his final bow. As soon as the clapping had died down, he came directly to the piano and took one of her hands in both his own.

"Nice going," he said. "You did a fine job."

"I'll say she did!"

Julie looked around surprised. The girl who had spoken was Mary De Angelis, whose brother had been beaten by George in the fight.

"Th-thank you," she stammered, but her voice was drowned in the commotion as other players gathered around to express their admiration and gratitude.

Julie's fame spread. People she hardly knew smiled at her in the corridors of the school—her school now, because she had made it a real contribution. And Dave Ross stopped to congratulate her!

A few days after the concert she came upon Doris Regan walking home from school alone. Why, she's never with Bets any more, Julie thought, and she wondered why this had not come to her notice before. Certainly she was aware of Bets' attachment to Beverly Blake, for it was Bets and Bev, Bets and Bev, all over the place. Some people said Bets was riding on Beverly's coat tails, but whether that was true or not, Julie saw now that Doris had been deserted as definitely as she herself had been. On an impulse of pity, she hurried to catch up to her old friend.

"Hello, Doris," she said.

Doris turned toward the voice and her eyes lit up. "Oh, hi, Julie."

"How've you been?" Julie shifted her books as they walked along.

"Okay. You?"

"Fine, thanks," Julie answered.

There was an uncomfortable pause.

Doris said, "You're getting famous, Julie."

"No, I'm not. Not really."

They walked a few more steps in uneasy silence. Then, abruptly, Doris began to talk.

"I guess I was pretty horrible to you last fall. I didn't want to do it, but you see, Bets said—well, she knew there were sororities at school and she thought we'd have a better chance if we—if there were only two of us."

"Oh," Julie said. "Yes."

"You know how they are. It isn't only what you're like yourself; it's who your friends . . ." Doris jerked her head, scowling. "No, I mean, it would have been a miracle if they liked all three of us."

"Well . . ." Julie did not know what to say.

"I'm sorry, Julie. I really am. I guess it serves me right that I didn't make a sorority."

"Maybe you'll make one next year."

"I don't know. I'm not very popular."

They had come to the Regans' house and they stood there tongue-tied again. Julie twisted her beads. "I'd better get home."

"Julie! Come on in. You haven't been to my house in ages."

Julie looked at the house in which she had spent so many happy hours, and at the girl with whom she had become so constrained. Doris' fingers were kneading the edges of her books, and her face looked anxious. Julie was sorry for her, but she simply could not go back to the place she had once been.

"Thanks," she said, "but I can't today. I honestly have to go home." She smiled and raised one hand in a farewell gesture. " 'Bye."

"Good—bye."

Julie heard the prolonged word but she could no longer see the troubled face, for she had started on.

7

"ARE YOU SURE YOU DON'T WANT TO GO TO CAMP THIS summer?" Dr. Brownell set down his coffee cup and raised inquiring eyebrows toward his daughter.

"No, honestly, I don't. It's nice here," Julie said.

It certainly was nice this June morning with the sun pouring over the breakfast table and the trees beyond the windows full-leaved and motionless. There was not a sound except the faint swish of traffic from the street below.

Mother said, "Better send in her application, anyway. She may want to go when the time comes."

"No, I won't." Most of Julie's friends would be home this summer and there had been talk of picnics, trips to the beach, things like that.

"It would be good for you," Daddy urged. "There won't be much for you to do around here."

"There'll be enough. And I want to work on piano. A singer ought to be able to accompany herself when she practices." From the corner of her eye, Julie watched for her father's reaction, but his smile was enigmatic.

Mother quickly changed the subject. "Isn't it time you started for school?"

"I guess." Julie excused herself from the table. "See you later."

Walking down the stairs, she wondered why her father wanted to send her to a Negro camp, he who had urged her all along to make friends with all races. What would Lorraine Hall think of such deliberate isolation?

At the thought of Lorraine, Julie frowned. Something was dreadfully wrong with the girl, but what? Why did she fluctuate between listlessness and those furious bursts of activity which sent her to scrubbing floors already clean, to shampooing hair that already glistened? What made her act so indifferent when Julie went to the Halls'?

Only once in the past weeks had she warmed to Julie, and then she had made a strange remark. Marilyn had gone down to the street to round up the boys, and they were alone in the Halls' kitchen. Lorraine, apathetically pouring hot water into the dishpan, suddenly banged the teakettle against the edge of the sink.

"Julie. Take care of Marilyn, will you?"

"Marilyn?" Why did she need help, the girl who was always so carefree, who had already leaped ahead of Julie into the exalted world of girls who have dates?

"She's like my father." Lorraine reached back to set the kettle onto the stove. "They both get discouraged easily, and then they won't make any effort. My father isn't

stupid, Julie. He could hold jobs if he tried, but his reaction to prejudice is just to give up. I'm afraid Marilyn
will do the same thing."

"She won't." Julie picked up a dish towel. "She's going
to be an artist."

"I hope so. I was going to help her, but now . . . Go
on into the front room, Julie. There's no reason for you to
do our dishes."

"I don't mind," Julie said, but Lorraine was firm.

"I'd rather work alone."

Baffled by her dismissal, Julie was glad to hear Marilyn and her brothers at the front door.

"Is Lorraine mad at me?" she asked Marilyn a few days
later.

"No, I'm sure she isn't. Not just you, anyway. She's
moping all the time lately." Marilyn did not know why.

She's unhappy about something, Julie thought, and she
longed to be the one to comfort her. But the girl made her
too uneasy these days, uneasy and rudderless as well. Lorraine had always been the strong one.

But now Julie had another problem on her mind, she and
everyone else at school. Exams. She was a good student,
but there was always the chance of tests filled with the
very questions she could not answer, nor could she be im-
mune to the tension in the air. Anna was keyed up to fever
speed; boys and girls brought their books to lunch; one
afternoon Julie heard Bev Blake refuse a date so she could
study.

Only Marilyn seemed unaffected.

"Aren't you at all jittery?" Julie asked her.

It was lunch hour and they were sitting in the shade of the tree where they had first met. Marilyn leaned against its rough bark. "Why worry? If I pass, I pass; if I don't, I don't. It won't do any good to lose sleep over it."

"Marilyn." Julie leaned toward her. "Did Lorraine flunk any of her college exams?" Could this be what was troubling her?

"Not her, I'm sure. My sister never flunks."

Neither will I, Julie determined, and she pitched into her books harder than ever, pushed herself to the ultimate straight through the oppressive heat of exam week. When the last test was finished, it left her completely let down and all afternoon she wandered around the house, unable to settle anywhere. After dinner when her father said he had to make a call, she decided to go along for the ride, but halfway to their destination, changed her plans.

"Let me out here, will you, Daddy? I think I'll go down to Marilyn's for a while." She had not been there for two weeks and perhaps, by this time, Lorraine's mood had worn off.

On the Halls' street the sidewalks were crowded with people who had brought chairs outside or were sitting on the steps to get a breath of air. Children ran among them, undaunted by the weather. Julie looked for the Hall boys, who were usually in the thick of any activity, but they were nowhere around, nor were their parents among the older people strung along the walk. Could something be wrong?

She hurried into the apartment house and up the stairs. On the Halls' landing she stopped and her heart began to thump, for sounds of moaning came through the thin walls. She half-turned back toward the stairway, tempted to retreat. But maybe they needed help. With a tight fist she knocked on the door.

Abruptly the moans stopped. There was dead silence. Then footsteps. The door opened a crack and Marilyn peered expectantly into the hall. When she saw Julie, she slumped. "Oh. It's you."

"What's wrong?" Beyond Marilyn, Julie had caught a glimpse of the Hall family huddled together in a tight little group. But one person was missing. "Where's Lorraine?"

"She's . . ." Marilyn glanced back over her shoulder, then stepped into the hall and pulled the door shut behind her. "She's gone."

Julie's fear deepened. "Where?"

"That's just it. We don't know. Maybe we never will." Marilyn's head and eyes moved around in quick jerks as if someone might be after her. She lowered her voice almost to a whisper. "Julie, she's passed."

Julie stared at her friend in disbelief. This couldn't be true. Lorraine was light enough to pass as white, but she would never hurt her family by leaving them forever, cutting all ties, all communication, lest the secret of her race be discovered.

"Marilyn, she couldn't!"

"She didn't even say good-bye." Marilyn clapped her hands over her face to catch a spurt of tears.

Julie put an arm around her and pulled her down to sit on the stairs. "Then surely she hasn't gone for good."

"She has. My mother had a letter this morning. Lorraine must have mailed it before she left."

A letter. Lorraine's moodiness. That legacy of the guardianship of Marilyn. It must be true.

"If we'd only known!" Marilyn said. "We might have stopped her. We might have found a way for her to go to college."

"But didn't she go to night school?"

"Only for one course a semester. The family always needed the money."

Julie had noticed but never fully considered the Halls' poverty. Could she have helped? Wouldn't Daddy . . . Suddenly she saw the face of her father as plainly as if he were there and she cried out, "But how could she leave her family this way?"

"I don't know! I don't know! It was her job, mostly. The promotions always went to white girls."

"I—see." Was this what Daddy meant about a musical career? Would the laurels always go to a white singer, regardless of talent, regardless of hard work?

Marilyn's breath caught in a sob and Julie tried to comfort her. "Marilyn, maybe she'll come back. Don't they sometimes do that?"

"Not Lorraine. Once she decides . . . Julie, it's as if she was dead!"

"Don't say that!" But Julie knew that it could not be denied. And there was nothing more to be said unless . . . "Should I go and speak to your folks?"

"Oh, no! They'd kill me if they knew I'd told. But I had to talk to someone." Marilyn stood up and wiped her arm across her eyes. "I'd better go in."

Julie watched as she opened the door just wide enough to squeeze through, and again she heard the weeping. Tears sprang to her own eyes and she ran down the stairs and into the street, dodging through the crowds, oblivious to everything but the saddened family she had left behind.

How could Lorraine have done this to them? Lorraine, who had always seemed so valiant, whom Julie had used as a model for so many months. How many times had she asked herself what Lorraine would do in this or that situation? How many times had her actions grown from the answer to that question? By the time she came, panting, to the bus stop, Julie was choked with anger, for she felt betrayed.

For endless minutes she paced back and forth. Where was the bus? She wanted to get home to her father and mother, to feel herself close to them as she had in the past, never to leave them again.

Eventually the bus lumbered into view. As it stopped in front of her, Julie moved down from the curb and had one foot on the lower step before she remembered that her wallet was at home.

"Oh dear!" She stepped back. "I can't get on. I have no money."

"Why'n'tcha make up yer mind?" The driver slammed the door in her face and drove off, leaving her with the fumes from his exhaust hot in her nostrils.

Abashed, too disheartened to start the long walk home, she had not budged from the gutter when a car drew up beside her and its door opened. Daddy! Julie jumped in and buried her face in his shoulder.

He put his arm around her. "Julie, what is it?"

"It's Lorraine. She's passed."

Julie felt his arm stiffen but he spoke quietly. "Passed."

"She doesn't even care what happens to her family."

"Julie, we can't park here. We'll talk about it as we go along."

Dr. Brownell put the car into gear and as they drove through the summer dusk, Julie, snuggled against him, told him the whole story, holding back neither her anger nor her hurt.

To her astonishment Daddy seemed to sympathize with Lorraine. "Don't be too hard on her. I'd rather have seen her stay with us, but this step takes courage too. And she has that. I've known her all her life and I've watched her fight. Against too much responsibility, poverty . . ."

"And race." It was the first time Julie had spoken the word.

"And race," Dr. Brownell agreed sadly.

A picture flashed before Julie's eyes, clear as a stereopticon, all her white friends, each one with a grin on her face, every grin a leer. The pain of all their slights rose into one concentrated sensation and her revulsion shifted from Lorraine to them and to the people like them, whose thoughtless cruelty had forced Lorraine's decision. She shuddered, as if to shake them off.

"Daddy?"

"Yes, Julie?"

"Did you send in that application for camp?"

"I sent it two weeks ago. Your mother thought you might change your mind."

"Well, I have changed it." Julie sat up straight, her lips compressed into a determined line. Let them have their picnics. Let them go to the beach. She would not be with them, not this summer nor ever again.

8

"That we may perfectly love Thee and worthily magnify Thy Holy Name . . ."

Julie kept her head reverently bowed during the prayer, but when the choral response began, she peeked from under her veil for another look at the choir. No, there were no young people among them.

At a nudge from her mother, she sat up and grinned sheepishly. Engrossed in her study of the singers, she had not noticed that everyone else was done with prayer, nor heard the scrape and shuffle as the congregation pulled its hymn books from the racks.

When they rose to sing, she tucked her arm through her mother's and gave it a squeeze. Camp had been wonderful but it was so good to be home again!

"Onward Christian soldiers . . ."

For once Julie did not join the singing wholeheartedly but let her eyes dart here and there at the people about her. Without actually turning around she could see only two or three of her own age. Perhaps church was not the answer after all.

"Like a mighty army . . ."

Mother had been surprised to see her at breakfast so early, eager to go to church, for they had talked half the night catching up on the summer's news. But this was the haven to which Julie's thoughts had turned during the long happy days at camp.

In the brisk mountain air, in the hours on the lake and along the woods trails, the shock of Lorraine's passing had worn off. Julie had come home restored, but her resolve remained strong. There would be no more of what George called bowing and scraping, no further attempt to find her way into a world which could only stab and wound. She would sing, but for her own people; she would make friends, but among those of her own race as she had at camp. What better place to do these things than at her church?

But if there were no young people in the choir or congregation? There were, though. During the long sermon Julie perused the church calendar and saw a notice which might unlock the door. Youth Fellowship. They were to hold a dance in the church basement this coming Friday.

She raised her head and tried to attend the minister's words, but her mind wandered off into a glorious daydream. She saw herself make a triumphant entry into the party, heard the excited whispers, "Who is she?" "Who is she?" accepted bids to dance from boy after boy.

The preacher's voice rose to an oratorical peak and it brought her back to earth, back to the real Julie, tongue-tied and awkward in the presence of boys, standing at the side of the room alone. Maybe Marilyn Hall would come with her.

The Halls had no phone, so Julie went to their apartment the next afternoon, but no one was at home. By Tuesday, when she started to school, she had more than just Marilyn on her mind. This was the day for which she had planned so carefully, the day on which a new Julie would emerge, armored by the strength of her own independence.

As she neared the school, many people called out greetings and she found herself able to respond quite casually. It was not hard at all. She did not have to be unfriendly just because she did not want to be friends; beneath a smile she could develop a core of obduracy which would satisfy even her father's requirements.

Her bubble of complacency exploded inside the gate when Anna came tearing across the campus with a joyous squeal. "Julie! It's super to see you! How are you, anyway? When did you get back? Did you have a good time at camp? I have so much to tell you!"

Warmth rose unbidden in Julie's chest and burst out into laughter. "Anna! Anna! One thing at a time."

Anna grinned. "Yakety-yak Jensen. That's me. Oh." Her glance went beyond Julie. "There's Louis Stevens. I have to go." Her lips nearly brushed against Julie's ear and she spoke in an undertone. "He's been dating me this summer. Isn't that dreamy?" Before Julie could answer, she was gone.

Julie peered over her shoulder to where Anna approached Louis with seeming nonchalance. Why had she thought it would be easy to give up her former friends?

She started in search of Marilyn, but Marilyn found her first. She came up from behind and, with a squeal much like Anna's, clapped both hands over Julie's eyes. "Guess who?"

"Superman." Julie turned around. "Marilyn, what—oh, a pony tail. I wouldn't have known you." It made her look older.

"Like it?"

"It's keen."

"I declare, I've missed you, Julie." Then, like Anna, Marilyn spotted a fellow. "Hey, there's Clem Atwood. Let's go talk to him."

"You go."

"Come on." Marilyn pulled Julie toward a boy with whom she was plainly on the chummiest of terms.

Julie stood by and studied Marilyn's technique. What did she do that made her seem so much more alive than usual? She stood still, yet her whole body seemed to be in motion; she only smiled, yet her whole face seemed to be alight.

The school bell interrupted her speculation, and she was caught up in the mob that shoved toward the door. Inside the building she was flooded with a sense of homecoming. There was the familiar smell of newly oiled floors, the remembered scurry and push, the ease with which she could find her way around. More than these were the frequent greetings of "Hi, Julie" that marked her progress through the corridors. Perhaps she could never fully detach herself, for this was her school.

Toward noon Anna caught up with her as she left a class. "Excuse me for walking out on you, Julie. He didn't ask me for a date, either!"

"Maybe he'll ask you later."

"I hope so. Hey, why don't we eat lunch together?"

"I can't, Anna. I mean, there's the bunch I always eat with."

"So we'll push the tables together," Anna said.

The others wouldn't like that, Julie knew, and she solved the problem by lunching with Marilyn under the tree. They both had so much to say that their words tumbled over each other's, and it was not until the crowds began to spill from the doors that they came to any pause.

"What's George doing?" Marilyn wanted to know.

"Nothing," Julie told her. "I guess he'll get a job later on."

"Well, he flunked out and all. I thought maybe he'd come back to school."

"Golly, no!" Julie said. At least she would not have that problem to contend with any more.

"He's—Julie! Will you look who's with Rickie Sheridan?"

"Bets Hampton!" Something akin to fear hollowed the pit of Julie's stomach. It was not the intimacy of their exchanged glances nor the way their hands touched as they walked along. It was the first time she had seen Rickie in the schoolyard apart from David Ross.

"She is pretty," Marilyn conceded.

"Mm." Why did it have to be Bets, of all people? Julie sighed. Poor David. "Everyone seems to be paired off this year."

"I know. You'd better get busy yourself, Julie."

"Who, me?" Julie's lips pulled up in a self-conscious smile.

"Why not?"

"Because . . ." Julie twisted the hem of her skirt between two fingers. "Marilyn, how do you talk to boys, anyway?"

Marilyn's peal of laughter sent the blood rushing to Julie's face. "I dunno. You just talk. That's all."

Just talk. It sounded so easy. "I was going to ask you, Marilyn. There's a dance at my church next Friday. Will you go with me?"

"A dance? Am I invited?"

"It said all young people."

"Sure. I'd love to go." Marilyn smiled at some secret thought. "I can wear my new dress."

"What's it like?"

"You've seen it, I guess. It's not really new. Lorraine left me her white jersey."

"Lorraine?" Julie moved closer to Marilyn. "Have you heard . . ."

Marilyn shook her head and began to gather the lunch papers. "Let's walk around. See who's here."

All week Julie looked forward to the party, half scared half excited. She bought a new dress herself, gold sheer wool with a pleated skirt, and had her hair shaped so that it cupped her head like a little cap. On Friday when she was ready to go, she was confident she looked her best.

Dr. Brownell drove Marilyn and her to the church and there even Marilyn had an attack of cold feet. "Are you sure we're invited?"

"Yes, I'm sure." Julie stared at the closed door.

"Why don't we go in then?" Marilyn made no move to start.

"I guess we'd better."

They might have been there indefinitely had not a boy and girl come up behind them.

"Hello," said the girl. "You coming to the party?"

"We'd like to," Julie said.

"Good. I'm Lena Talbott, president of Youth Fellowship. And this is Slim Watkins."

Julie introduced Marilyn and herself and Slim raised a loose-jointed hand. "Hiya."

"We may as well go in." Lena moved toward the door and just in time, Slim leaped forward to open it.

"Enter," he said with a wide sweep of his arm.

In the light that flooded from the lobby, Lena turned

to smile at the girls. "It's nice you came early. You'll have more time to get acquainted."

Down in the basement they found a handful of boys and girls clustered around a decrepit record player. When they saw Lena and Slim, one of them called out, "Say! This thing isn't working so good."

"Let papa see." Slim joined those tinkering with the player, while Lena made introductions.

"Why, I know Julie." It was a senior from her school. "Do you go to Hadley High, too?" she asked Marilyn.

As others arrived Julie recognized a few more upperclassmen from school and the Burkes, who came to chaperon, were acquaintances of her parents. Looking around at all the dark faces, it occurred to her that, except for the presence of boys, this group was much like the one at camp, and by the time they were ready to try the record player again, she felt quite at home.

"Listen, now." Slim snapped on the switch of the player and the creak of its machinery echoed loudly in the expectant silence. The record wobbled but the needle steadied it and at last the music of an outmoded popular tune blared into the room.

"Whassa matter with that?" Slim's torso bounced to the rhythm; his feet danced. "Let's go." He moved toward Lena.

Lena shook her head and Julie, near enough to hear her say, "Dance with one of the new girls," practically held her breath. But Slim chose a stranger.

That had been thoughtful of Lena, though. Julie glanced at the bony angular face, almost homely without its warm smile, and wondered if even Anna Jensen would have made such a gesture.

She saw that Marilyn was already dancing, one of the first girls to be chosen. And why not, for she was lovely in the white jersey. It was pulled in around her slim waist with a bright red cinch belt to match the bow in her hair and its wide skirt billowed and swirled as she flew over the floor.

"Who's that in the white dress?" someone asked.

"Marilyn Hall," Julie said.

"She's cute!"

One by one, the girls around Julie were picked off until she was part of an uncomfortably small group. A wallflower! It could be like this all evening. Urgently she eyed the boys slouched against the opposite wall in a group corresponding to her own. The record ended.

"They'll change partners now." The chubby girl next to Julie spoke hopefully, but no one came to claim her or Julie either. Marilyn, left alone, approached the stag line and in no time had pulled a fellow from its midst.

"She must have asked him!" Julie murmured.

"What?"

"Nothing. My friend is dancing with someone else."

"Yeah," said the chubby one without interest.

A few of the girls around them gave up and began to dance with each other. Among those left, conversation came to a dead stop. Julie felt as if her gold dress glittered, for most of the others wore cotton blouses and skirts. She fixed a tight smile onto her lips and wished heartily that she had stayed home.

After the second record, Lena called for a Paul Jones. Slim literally pushed the stags into the circle while Julie's little group joined it of their own accord.

"Grand right and left."

Right hand. Left hand. Please let me get a partner. Right hand. Left hand. There aren't enough boys to go around. Right hand. Stop! Julie's fingers felt the clammy grasp of a fellow no taller than herself.

He addressed the air just beyond her ear. "I guess we're partners."

"Yes."

Everyone around them started to dance, but the boy stood there, his hand seemingly stuck to hers. "I'm not much at dancing."

"Me, either," Julie said. "Shall we—try?"

Gingerly he put his arm around her and plowed forward. Plod. Plod. Plod-plod. Was it her feet or his that were out of time? Their progress was marked with missteps; their words limited to apologies.

Plod-plod. Plod. Say something. Get him to talk.

"My name's Julie."

"Mine's Joe."

That ended the conversation. Plod . . . The record wailed like a foghorn and died a mournful death. There was a mad rush to the player, but no amount of jiggling and whacking would get it started again.

"What'll we do now?"

"Games?"

"Sure. Sure. Ring around the Rosy."

"Can't anyone play the piano?"

"Julie Brownell can."

Marilyn! Marilyn Hall! Why did you say that? I don't want to be conspicuous.

"Who's Julie Brownell?"

"Right there." All eyes followed Marilyn's pointing finger.

"Come along, Julie." Slim had her arm and was propelling her toward the battered upright.

"But—but I can't play popular music."

"You gotta." He plopped her firmly onto the piano stool, thrust a sheet of music before her and stood back with folded arms, like a judge. "Now."

In a daze Julie struck a few tentative chords.

"Try the chorus." Slim bent to turn a page.

Julie ran through the chorus much in the style of Paderewski's *Minuet* and glanced up under her lashes at Slim's shaking head.

"Swing it, can'tcha?" he urged. "Like you was dancin'."

"I'll—see." Like dancing. Under the piano Julie's feet tapped out the rhythm and the movement flowed up into her shoulders and down to her hands. The harmony was unimportant; she thought only of the beat. Why! This was fun. Lots of fun. Shoulders and head swinging, one foot thumping on the pedal, Julie lost herself in the tempo.

"You've got it!" Slim grabbed her shoulders and planted an unexpected kiss on top of her head. In almost the same movement, he turned away and with snapping fingers and shuffling feet, danced into Marilyn's arms.

For nearly two hours Julie swung from one piece of music to another and back to the first. A few of the wall-flowers came to stand around her, and after them the reluctant stags. They began to sing and gradually the dancers joined them until, by popular request, she switched to songs like *I Been Workin' on the Railroad* and *Dinah, Won't You Blow.*

"Come and get it!" The refreshment committee shouted in unison to make itself heard over the racket, and the party moved toward the long table in a mass. Julie felt a pair of hands on her elbows as Slim lifted her to her feet and pushed her, laughing, after the crowd. She helped herself to cake and punch and found a chair next to Marilyn.

But she scarcely had time to eat because everyone pelted her with questions. Why hadn't she been around before? How had she learned to play so well? Where did she go to school? It was almost as exciting as the daydream.

All too soon it was time to break up. While they were getting their wraps, Lena thanked her for her help, and Slim, easing Lena's arms into her coat, grinned over her shoulder at Julie. "Now, don't you get lost again, girl."

"I won't."

"You, either." Slim reached out to yank at Marilyn's pony tail.

"Ouch! Slim!" Marilyn giggled.

Julie giggled, too, just because she was happy. Maybe she had not made any conquests, but she had had a wonderful time. Her first boy-girl party had been a success.

9

"So you want to be a singer." Miss Adams, the new music teacher, rested one arm on the piano top and regarded Julie thoughtfully.

"Yes, I do. I always have. Do you think I—can?" Julie clutched her books with tight fingers. It had taken her weeks to drum up courage to ask this attractive young woman's advice. She simply could not stand it if the answer were no.

Miss Adams picked up a pile of music and tapped the edges to evenness. "I don't know you well yet, so I can't tell whether you have the stamina, the capacity for hard work. But as far as your voice goes, I think you definitely have the talent."

"Do you really?" Julie practically shrieked with relief, forgetting the other members of the glee club who were filing past her toward the door. Miss Williams' indifference to her ambition had formed a gnawing doubt in her mind.

Miss Adams nodded. "How old are you, Julie?"

"Fifteen."

"You have time then. That's a bit young to start voice training."

"But it's so long to wait." Julie did not tell Miss Adams that she also had to win over her father. "Isn't there anything I can do in the meantime?"

Miss Adams seemed to be concentrating on the music in her hands. "Voice lessons are expensive, you know."

"I can manage. I'll manage somehow," Julie vowed.

Miss Adams laid down the music with a decisive gesture. "Send for the catalogue of a good music school. Juilliard, for instance. I'll go over it with you to see what courses you ought to take now."

"I will. I'll do it today. Thank you, Miss Adams. Thank you."

Julie hurried toward the door. The room had long since emptied, so she was surprised to find Anna in the corridor.

"Hi," Anna said.

In her excitement Julie dropped the protective reserve she had so carefully built up over the past weeks. "Anna! Miss Adams thinks I can sing."

"Did you need someone to tell you that?"

"I mean be a singer," Julie explained. "Miss Williams didn't seem so sure."

"Oh, her!" Anna said scornfully. "It's a good thing she retired. Miss Adams may be young but she knows more now than Miss Williams could ever learn."

"She's wonderful!" Julie sighed happily as they walked down the corridor.

"Julie," Anna said. "Reason I waited for you, I wanted to ask you. Is anything wrong?"

Julie snapped to wariness. "Of course not."

"But you never come for Cokes any more. I thought maybe you were mad at me or something."

"Are you crazy?" Julie's voice reflected her embarrassment.

"Well, I didn't know." Anna pulled at her sorority pledge ribbons as if remembering her unfortunate remark on the first day she had worn them. "Sure I'm glad, Julie. I mean, if you aren't asked to join a sorority, you always have to wonder what's wrong with you."

Julie recovered her poise. "It's just that I'm so busy." She counted her activities on her fingers. "Glee club, church choir, piano practice, Youth Fellowship . . ."

"I didn't know you were in Youth Fellowship." Anna opened the door and they both went out, squinting in the bright midautumn sunlight. "I'm on the social committee of mine."

"Truly? Me, too. Well, not regularly, but last week we gave a dinner to raise money for a new record player and I was in charge of setting tables."

"A dinner? Say, that's an idea. We have to raise some money too."

On the oval below the school, the track boys were at practice, their long legs graceful as dancers', the pad-pad of their feet sending out a rhythmic pattern of sound.

"Wow!" Anna said. "Did you see Rickie Sheridan shoot ahead of Dave Ross?"

"Mm." What had happened to David's rocket speed?

"Bets Hampton's practically going steady with Rickie these days."

"I know." Julie also knew that Bets had begun to cause a rift between Rickie and David as she had between Doris and herself.

"How does she do it, Julie? Just snag the most popular guy around. Like that." Anna snapped her fingers.

"You tell me!" Julie spoke with feeling. "I can't even get one to look at me once."

The girls' eyes met in an understanding glance and Anna reached for Julie's arm. "Come to The Hangout. Won't you?"

"I can't. Not this afternoon. Maybe some other time."

"Okay. I have to go. The bunch'll be waiting. So long."

" 'Bye." Julie watched Anna leave and the old longing welled up within her. If only Anna could be taken separately! More than anyone Julie knew, she seemed to feel the same way about things, to share the same uncertainties. Marilyn, with a different fellow to take her home from Youth Fellowship each Sunday, could never understand what it meant to be timid with boys. Nor, for that matter, could Julie comprehend Marilyn's lack of determination. How, for instance, could she have withdrawn from sketch club without an apparent qualm? Surely her reason, that she could not afford the field trips, was only an excuse.

Julie turned to go but her attention was arrested by the scene on the track oval. She saw David step out onto the grass and watched as he rubbed his head and shoulders with a towel and bent to pick up his sweat shirt. By that time Rickie had run once more around the track and he too dropped out to speak to David.

They must be arguing. Rickie scowled and gesticulated and David's head, emerging from his sweat shirt, jerked back and forth in a strong negative gesture. Julie could hear their voices but caught no words until David swung away from the oval and Rickie yelled after him, loud enough for the whole world to hear, "Quitter!" David did not turn back but came toward the steps, feet stamping, eyes glued to the ground.

Julie was shaken by the strength of her reaction. The admiration she had always felt for David, the secret yearning she had cherished since the day he had called her by name in church, merged into an all-consuming feeling of identity. Rickie and David had been friends and Bets had come between them. No one knew better than she what this could mean nor realize how much of David's anger sprang from hurt. Like a mother hen, she leaped to his defense and with complete self-forgetfulness called out to him as he passed.

"David?"

Barely glancing at her, he grunted, " 'Lo," and went on. Humiliation pricked her cheeks with a thousand needles and she, too, walked off with lowered eyes. How could she have thought that a wheel like David Ross would want her friendship? Then, as so often happened with her, self-condemnation flew out into anger. Just let David Ross ever try to speak to her again!

And yet, not two weeks later, when David turned up at a Youth Fellowship meeting, the muscles around her heart contracted and she stopped right in the middle of a sentence. Though she rallied quickly, Lena, who had not missed her confusion, looked around to discover the cause.

"New fellow." With her usual tact, Lena did not mention Julie's momentary distraction.

"Yes. He goes to my school," Julie told her. "His name's David Ross."

"Do you know him well enough to introduce me?" Lena asked. "It'll make it easier to welcome him."

"I—a—okay."

Julie's introduction was high-pitched and a little too loud. She stood by smiling stiffly while Lena talked to David, but soon he was surrounded by boys who had met him through inter-school athletics, and the girls withdrew.

His presence made her self-conscious and as she played for the hymns, her fingers seemed all thumbs. She had been chosen to read the Scriptures for the evening and though she had practiced faithfully, her words came out weak and wavery. Why must she do everything badly, tonight of all nights?

After the meeting everyone hung around to talk for a while and Julie, in the midst of a group, kept stealing surreptitious glances at David until he caught her at it. Flustered, she turned away, but he sauntered toward her and spoke her name.

"Julie?"

"Hi, David."

"I wanted to thank you for introducing me tonight."

"That's all right. Looks as if practically everyone knew you, anyway."

"Some of the fellows. You know how it is. When you're in athletics, you get around."

"Yes."

The crowd had begun to thin out and Marilyn, with Slim Watkins at her side, stopped to say good night. "Slim's taking me home." Her eyes were shining. She had hoped for Slim ever since they had found out he was not Lena's personal property.

Julie watched them leave and said, "I'd better get started too."

"Anyone walking you?" David asked.

"Well—no."

"How about me?" He grinned.

"Oh. Thank you."

Julie's spirits soared until she found herself alone with David on the street. Then the old stiffness came over her as she sought for words. But David was not shy.

"Hey, that was nice what you said before. All those fellows recognizing me."

"I guess everyone knows you, David."

"Yeah?" He sounded pleased. "You seem to be somebody yourself around there."

"Just because I play the piano?"

"Not only that. You read the Scriptures—you're in with the president . . ."

"Lena's friendly with everyone." Actually Julie had already become a leader in this group, and she could not help being glad that David had noticed.

"Where do you live, Julie?"

"Don't you know?" She was uneasy again. What would he say when he found how far he had to take her? "The last house on Washburne Avenue."

"No kiddin'. Do you walk way out there every Sunday?"

"No, I take the bus."

David jingled the change in his pocket. "So we'll take the bus."

As they rode along, he talked mostly of athletics and Julie was content to listen. Once he asked if she had been in Youth Fellowship long and she said, "Just this year."

"How come? You could have joined when you were a freshman."

"Why didn't you?" she countered.

"I dunno. Busy, I suppose." Something in his tone, in the way his eyes shifted from hers, made Julie wonder if his reasons for coming to Youth Fellowship now were the same as her own.

When they alighted from the bus, she said, "It's good you're an athlete. There are a million steps up to my house."

"Bet I could run all the way," David bragged.

"You couldn't!"

"Want to see?" He tore up the steps with Julie after him until she called, "David! Wait!"

He did wait and reached for her hand to pull her up beside him. For a second they stood together, breathless and laughing, but David quickly dropped her hand and they moved on.

"You're a softie," he teased.

"I am not!"

In sight of the house he whistled. "Gee! A mansion!"

"It's not all that big." Julie thought of the small houses out on the edge of town where David lived, and hoped that he would not be awed by the size of hers.

When they turned the last bend in the stairway, the light from the living room flooded over them and they could see Dr. Brownell near the window, bent over a book.

"That your dad waiting up for you?" David asked.

"He never goes to bed early." Julie wondered whether she was supposed to ask David in.

"What does he do, anyway? For work, I mean."

"He's a doctor," Julie said.

"Yeah? My dad's sexton of St. Paul's. Biggest church in town."

"Is he really?" Julie responded to the pride in his voice.

"Yeah. He has an assistant too."

"Will you—would you like to come in?"

"Uh-uh. Not tonight. I'd better get rollin'."

"Well—thanks a lot, David."

"That's okay. 'Night, Julie. I'll see you."

"Yes." Julie stood where she was while David ran down the stairway. Then she dashed into the house, bursting with the news that he had seen her home.

But it was not until she got into bed that she really began to relive the evening, gesture by gesture, word by word. If only there were someone with whom she could share this precious experience! You couldn't tell all the little details to a father or mother. People that old would think it sounded silly.

Anna Jensen! She was the one who would understand. Julie pushed herself up to lean against the headboard and, though still wrapped in awareness of David, let her thoughts wander off to Anna. To her unself-conscious friendliness, to her outgoing warmth, to her identification with others. What if once in a while she inadvertently said or did some little thing that hurt? Julie asked herself whether in avoiding the small heartaches, she was not also giving up something big and worth while, the natural give and take of real friendship.

She slid down into her bed again and snuggled under the blankets. When at last she fell asleep, she was still planning the words she would use to tell Anna all about what had happened tonight.

⁕ 10 ⁕

MARILYN TORE ACROSS THE SCHOOLYARD AND WAGGLED A finger in Julie's face. "Julie Brownell, you big fake!"

"What do you mean, fake?"

Marilyn grinned. "You don't know how to get along with boys. Not much. You only got Dave Ross to take you home last night."

"How did you know?" Julie was puzzled.

"News travels fast around here. Julie, do you know that Dave Ross has never even looked at a girl before?"

The words sounded familiar and, with a sudden sense of dismay, Julie remembered where she had heard them. "Marilyn, you wanted Dave. You told me the first time I saw you."

"That was a long time ago," Marilyn said. "Before I knew Slim."

"And Clem and Jim and Hank!" Julie laughed.

"Oh, well." Marilyn pushed back the hair which had blown across her face. "I may as well have fun."

As the weeks went by, Marilyn continued to have fun

with Clem and Jim and Hank and Slim, but Julie had less luck with Dave. At Youth Fellowship, along the corridors of the school, he often raised her hopes by seeking her out, but he did not take her home again until the night of the church Christmas party.

"That was three weeks ago," she told Anna one afternoon, "and he hasn't asked me since."

Anna finished her soda with a loud suck and an embarrassed, "Oh, 'scuse. But he must like you," she said. "He's always talking to you around school. Maybe he's shy."

"Not Dave Ross!" Not the boy who was sure of himself almost to the point of arrogance; whose self-confidence was constantly bolstered by praise. How he had been lionized at Youth Fellowship when, after his poor track season, he had broken a record in the county meet!

"Maybe he's upset about something." Anna picked up her paper napkin and started to tear its edges into fringe. "I may as well tell you, Julie. I heard that the basketball coach accused him of playing a one-man game and threatened to throw him off the team."

"But he's one of the best players!" Julie cried.

"Was. He and Rickie Sheridan were an unbeatable combination but they don't seem to click any more."

"Oh." Julie wished there were some way to tell Dave that you eventually recover from a broken friendship, but how could anyone show sympathy to a fellow who always covered his hurt?

"I have to go." Anna pushed back her glass.

"Me, too," Julie said. "Homework."

"Honestly, Julie. You're getting to be a regular brain."

A brain? While she waited for the bus, Julie wondered if it was her high position on the honor roll which had scared Dave off. But she had to maintain it, no matter what, to make sure that if Daddy should let her apply to Juilliard, her grades would be beyond question.

And surely, in the end, he would give his consent. According to the catalogue, admission to the school depended largely on a performance test, but the applicant's general knowledge of music was examined too. And her father had raised no objection when, at Miss Adams' suggestion, Julie had asked his permission to join a class in musical theory.

"But you'll have to pay for it yourself," had been his only condition.

"I will." It took most of her allowance but she did not care. It was such a relief to find at least one thing she could do in preparation while she waited for her voice to mature enough for serious study.

With this class added to a full school curriculum, Julie had a heavy schedule, but she did not have to work every minute. If only the pond would freeze over, perhaps she would see Dave there. Or would she? Last year he had always come skating with Rickie.

Toward the end of the week a cold snap froze the world solid, and again Julie became a part of the gay afternoons at the skating pond. She was never alone there, for as time had softened her bitterness, and Anna's loyal devotion restored her faith, she had gradually drifted back to her old crowd. But Dave did not show up.

"If you want him to go skating with you, ask him," Marilyn advised.

"Marilyn! I couldn't do that!"

"Why not, for lands' sake?"

"Wouldn't it be sort of—pushy?"

"Nuts," said Marilyn. "That's how I got a date with George."

"George? My cousin?"

"Didn't I tell you? It was right after your carol party this year. But I'll have to admit he hasn't called since."

"He's probably broke, Marilyn. He quit working in his father's store right after Christmas." It had been his fourth job since June.

"It doesn't matter. I have enough boy friends. But what about you and Dave?"

Julie thought for a moment. "I couldn't ask him. Really."

But Marilyn had implanted an idea, and the next time Dave stopped to chat and asked Julie what she had been up to lately, she surprised herself with her reply. "Mostly skating. Why don't you come along some time?"

"Say, I might at that. You dated up with anyone for tomorrow afternoon?"

"No, I'm—not." The girls would forgive her if she left them for a date.

"Well! We can go together then."

Julie had never had an experience like that of skating

with Dave. It was fun to learn the new steps he taught her, but she liked it best when he took both her hands and they moved together in the easy rhythm of a slow dance or so fast it felt like flying. If only he would join in the games with the others!

"Why not?" she asked him. "The whips are simply hysterical."

"Who wants to be hysterical?"

"You did last year," she reminded him.

"Hey! Did you notice me around here last year?"

As if she had not noticed him from the first day of high school! Nevertheless, his exclusiveness embarrassed her and she was almost glad he did not come to the pond every day. Paradoxically, on the Saturday morning when she and Anna found the ice turned to slush, she worried that she might not see him any more.

"What you ought to do is get on a committee with him." Anna sat down on a bench and dropped her skates to the ground. "I've seen a lot of Louis since we started to work on our Youth Fellowship dinner."

Julie joined Anna on the bench. "How's it going? Your dinner, I mean."

"Pretty well. If we only had an idea for entertainment. You know, something different. What did you do at your dinner?"

"Not much," Julie said. "Marilyn's friend, Slim, did a tap dance and four of us sang in a quartet."

"Julie!" Anna sat up straight and grabbed at Julie's

sleeve. "There's my idea. How would you like to sing for us?"

"Me?" A pleased smile formed on Julie's lips, but she felt all scary inside. "But I don't belong to your church."

"So what? You'll be a guest artist, Julie! Come on. I want to get to a phone and tell Louis."

"Hey, wait a minute. I didn't say I'd do it." Julie could envision an audience of adults, hostile like Bets or sweetly condescending like Beverly Blake.

"You've got to," Anna said. "Just think, Julie. When you're a great opera star, I can say, 'She's a friend of mine. Sang her first solo at my church.' "

Her first solo! There would be other audiences, each one to be won over, before all of whom she must break down the bars of prejudice through the common bond of music. What were the words her father had used? *Live so that they can see your worth.* Daddy would approve of this. It might even be the one last push to win him to her side.

"All right, Anna. I'll do it," she said.

Excitement mingled with the scariness now and carried her through the day, through her mother's apprehension about her singing at a white church and her father's, "You may be hurt, Julie, but I guess you'll have to find out for yourself." When Dave called and invited her to go to the movies, it seemed to fit the unreality of a dreamlike day.

But Dave destroyed the dream. For most of the evening, Julie abandoned herself to the pure pleasure of being with him and it was not until they had started home on the bus that she said, "Guess what. I've been asked to sing at Anna Jensen's church."

"No kiddin'." Dave seemed amused. "I hope you said no."

"Why should I?" Julie asked.

"Take my advice." Dave emphasized his words with a pointing finger. "Stick to your own church."

"I will, but this is special. I'm to be a—guest soloist." Julie chuckled sheepishly at the imposing title, but Dave was dead serious.

"I mean it, Julie. It won't do you any good to hang around with those people. Believe me, I know."

"But Anna's one of my best friends." Julie was unaware that she spoke with a note of pride. "She asked me as a favor to her."

"Sure, sure. As long as you have something she wants, she's your buddy. Wait till she doesn't need you any more." Dave sounded bitter, and Julie, watching the set lines of his profile, tried to find words to soften him. But it was impossible to explain away Bets Hampton, and before she could think of anything to say, he turned to face her.

"Don't do it, Julie."

Julie faltered before the pleading in his eyes. "I—promised."

"Break it then." Dave put his hand over one of hers, and Julie very nearly forgot Anna and even her own career. But not quite.

"Listen," she said. "It isn't only Anna. I want to be a singer. I want it more than anything. This is a chance to prove that I can face a—an audience."

"Don't do it," Dave persisted and his hand tightened over hers.

Julie longed to agree, to please Dave, to bring back the smile that was just for her. The power of this impulse was so strong it made her taut to bursting, but beneath it was that other urge, deep as the bass notes of a chord, the goal toward which she must always strive.

"I have to do it, Dave," she said.

Dave withdrew his hand and moved away so that she could no longer feel his shoulder against hers. It was as if he had shut a door between them, except that Julie could feel his resentment seeping through. Surely this was too heavy a price to pay, to lose Dave when she had so nearly won him. But what else could she do? How could she explain a withdrawal of her promise to the father who had warned her that she might be hurt? No, she must sing at Anna's church, even if it meant the end of Dave.

"Here's your stop," Dave said. He helped her off the bus and as they climbed her stairway talked to her desultorily about impersonal matters. At her door he stuffed his hands into his pockets and seemed to wait for her to speak.

She said, "I had such a good time. Thanks a lot, Dave."

"Okay." Dave ran the toe of his shoe against the edge of

the doormat. "Look, Julie. It's not my affair, but if that's the kind of people you like, don't expect me to go along."

"But Dave. I have other friends."

"Yeah. Well." Dave pulled one hand out of his pocket and tapped it lightly against Julie's arm. "S' long, Julie."

"Good—night." Julie reached out as if to stop him, but he was gone. For good, she was sure. She stood and listened to his footsteps growing fainter and fainter, until finally the sound was lost in the night.

11

ANNA AND HER COMMITTEE HAD DONE WELL IN SELLING
tickets to their dinner, and the tables were filled to the last
chair. Julie, seated between Mr. and Mrs. Jensen, pushed
her food around her plate and nervously watched the room-
ful of people who were to be her first audience.

A tap on her shoulder made her jump, but it was only
Anna with a steaming pitcher. "Coffee, Julie?"

"No, thanks. Well, yes. I guess I will." Daddy did not
approve of coffee for young people, but maybe it would
give her a much-needed shot in the arm.

As she sipped the hot bitter liquid, a withered little
woman with a fishlike mouth leaned across the table and
said, "I understand you're a friend of the Jensen girl."

"Yes, I am." Julie set down her cup.

"I think that's so nice," the woman gushed. "When I
was a girl, that sort of thing wouldn't have happened, but
the young people are so much more broadminded these
days."

There was no answer to that and Julie smiled politely
and made another attempt at her food.

"You don't eat." Mr. Jensen spoke with a slight accent. "Don't you like roast beef?"

"What a question, Papa!" Mrs. Jensen, too, had an accent, different from her husband's and more pronounced. "When we have to perform, we do not eat the food, no?"

"Yes, that's it." Julie liked Anna's stout, rather dowdy mother.

The little woman was at her again. "My dear, my friend says I have hurt your feelings. I didn't mean to. This is a Christian church and everyone is welcome here."

Once more Mrs. Jensen interceded. "We leave Julie alone, yes? She thinks now about her music."

"I really should." Julie opened her purse and took out the small cards on which she had printed her words in case stage fright should drive them from her mind. She went over and over them, all but humming the tunes, while the plates were changed and the ice cream served.

It was not until the tables were being cleared that she came back to her surroundings and noticed Anna and Louis beside the platform at one end of the room. Anna had a sheet of paper in her hand, the program, probably. Julie's heart banged against her ribs.

Think about something else, she told herself, about how well Anna is getting along with Louis, for instance. This train of thought took her naturally to David, whose coolness since the movie date had led her to avoid him. After all, who was he to tell her who her friends should be?

Anna climbed to the platform and Louis struck a dissonant chord on the piano to get attention. There was a scrape and shuffle as people turned their chairs to face the front of the room. Anna, flushed and a little shaky, started her opening speech. The program had begun!

It was impossible to think of anything else now, and Julie sat in tight apprehension through the speeches and the short skit until Anna came forward to make her last announcement.

"And now we come to the treat of the evening, our guest soloist, Miss Julie Brownell."

Julie worked her way through the tables and chairs, nodded at Anna's choir director who was to accompany her, and stepped to the platform. If she had been scared before, she was practically paralyzed now. She thrust her little cards behind her back to hide the trembling of her hands.

The old piano tinkled the opening phrase of *In My Garden*. Julie took one deep breath and began.

Horrors! What had happened to her voice? These warbled notes, could they be coming from her own throat? She quavered on almost automatically, tingling with prickles to the roots of her hair.

The audience applauded. Actually, they clapped more than they had for the speeches or the skit, but Julie, bowing graciously, wished they would stop so she could sing her next song and get it over.

The second selection went a little better than the first. The awful quiver was gone, but Julie knew she had never sung so poorly. When she was done, she wanted to run from the room but she walked back to her table, returning the smiles of the people she passed on the way. It was not until she was in her seat that she noticed the little cards, now damp in her hand. There were three cards and she had sung two songs. They had not asked for an encore!

Going home in the Jensens' car, Julie joined Anna's happy chatter about the success of the dinner, but underneath was the knowledge of her failure. What would she tell her parents?

When they asked her how it had gone, she decided on the truth. "Terrible," she said.

"Julie," Mother worried. "Was it the people? Did they make you feel uncomfortable?"

Julie skipped over the memory of fish-mouth. "No, it was me. I couldn't have done worse." She hardly dared look at her father.

"It was probably nerves," Dr. Brownell said. "I was afraid it would be too hard for you."

"But I have to get over nerves." Julie walked across the room and faced him squarely. "I have to learn how to control the tremolo when I'm scared. Daddy, I need training."

"Be patient, Julie. I told you we'd consider it when the time comes."

Yes, but what if he should still say no? Julie had been going along on the assumption that her father would relent, had been unable to believe that he would deny her what she wanted so much. Recently he had been impressed with her earnestness, her good report cards, her concentration on every detail that might forward her musical career. But why did he keep putting her off?

For the first time in over a year, Julie faced the fact that she could not rely on her father's backing. At the same time her failure at Anna's church made her more anxious than ever to assure herself of instruction. What if she should get a job? Surely Daddy would not withhold his consent if she could pay for her own lessons.

Surreptitiously she began to study the help-wanted ads, but no one was interested in a fifteen-year-old girl. At school she discussed the matter with everyone who had ever earned a cent. Baby sitting seemed to be the major occupation, but the rates paid did not compare with the price of a good voice teacher.

The problem was never far from her mind, but she was not particularly thinking about it the day she went on a cook-out with the glee club crowd. It was cold for late March and the girls were huddled around the fire waiting for the hamburgers to cook when someone asked Evvy Newton why she was not at her ballet class.

"It's no fun any more," Evvy grumbled. "The accompanist got independent and decided she needed Saturdays to be with her husband. And I hate dancing to scratchy records."

Accompanist? Saturdays? "Does your teacher want to hire a pianist for just that one day?" Julie asked.

Evvy's blue eyes widened as if in surprise. "Why I never thought of you! I'll ask her. I'll call her tonight."

On Monday morning Evvy reported that her ballet teacher was definitely interested and would like to see Julie at five-thirty that afternoon. "Her name's Miss Novikoff and she's at 32 South Main," Evvy said. "You walk up to the second floor."

Julie floated through the day in a happy daze. She tore home after school to change her clothes, thankful that it was Mother's Brownie Scout day so she could get out of the house without answering questions.

She was downtown way ahead of time and wandered along Main Street, stealing glances at her reflection in the store windows to be sure her stocking seams were straight and her slip not showing. At five-twenty-five she peeked at her pocket mirror and, satisfied that her lipstick was even, walked up the stairs of No. 32 and knocked on the door marked *Novikoff School of the Dance*.

A tall, bony woman opened the door and regarded Julie from enormous dark eyes. "Yes?" she said.

Julie cleared her throat. "How do you do? I'm Julie Brownell."

The woman seemed startled and showed no sign of recognition.

"I . . ." Julie wavered. "Evelyn Newton sent me. Are you Miss Novikoff?"

The woman nodded and pushed at her thick black bangs with a troubled gesture. "Come in."

Julie stepped into the small reception room but Miss Novikoff walked away and busied herself with the papers on her desk. "I do not know how to say. Evelyn did not tell me . . ."

"She said you wanted an accompanist," Julie said.

"Yes. Yes." Miss Novikoff dropped the papers and stepped around to lean against the desk. "My dear, I am a foreigner so I know this thing. People, they have the—almost the fear of someone who is not like themselves."

Julie's knees grew wobbly as the dancing teacher went on. "I need an accompanist. If you play, I take you gladly. But some of my mothers . . ." She shook her head. "No. This I cannot do."

"You mean . . ." Julie backed toward the door.

"Wait." Miss Novikoff reached for her pocketbook and fumbled around in its depths. "I am sorry you took this time to come here." She pulled out a bill and thrust it at Julie. "Please. You take this for your trouble."

"Oh no, Miss Novikoff. I couldn't. Thank you." Julie fled.

At home she found the house in a turmoil. Sarah Lou was on the couch and Dr. Brownell bent over her, was muttering, "Appendix." Mrs. Brownell was telephoning the hospital. Julie, alarmed, was diverted from her experience and later, when her mother asked where she had been, was able to answer with relative calm. "To see a friend of Evvy Newton's."

At school she merely told Evvy that Miss Novikoff had turned her down, but she was uncomfortable with her white friends, knowing that Evvy would discover and might repeat the whole story. Only a stubborn determination kept her with them, an urge to show that David, a need to prove to herself that she could take it. It was with this crowd that she went to the last basketball game of the season.

The game was a fiasco. Rickie and Dave seemed to be playing at cross purposes. Dave missed shot after shot and fouled out before the end of the first half. The team could not pull itself together as the score mounted steadily for the opponents.

Julie was among those who left right after the game since they had no dates for the dancing which followed. It was not until the next day, when Marilyn came up to spend Saturday afternoon, that she heard about the fight between Rickie and Dave.

"It was awful," Marilyn moaned. "In the locker room after the game, with the other team still around."

"Marilyn! Was Dave hurt?"

"No. The coach and some of the fellows pulled them apart. Seems Rickie accused Dave of throwing the game and Dave couldn't make him take it back."

Julie chewed her lip. If only she had tried to talk more to Dave! Maybe she could have helped him.

"Coach gave 'em both the dickens," Marilyn continued. "Told them they could either change their attitudes or not bother to show up for practice next year."

"Was Dave—did you see Dave?"

"Uh-uh." Marilyn sat down on the top porch step. "He's a nice kid, but I don't know. Some people think he's getting too braggy."

"He does not brag!" Julie glared at Marilyn, then flopped onto the steps and gazed out over the river. She had forgotten Dave's trouble in worry about her own and had neglected everyone else, really. Sarah Lou, still suffering from the effects of a ruptured appendix. Marilyn, who had lost a sister. She thought of Lorraine as she had last seen her there in the kitchen, and now she remembered that parting request. *Take care of Marilyn.*

She hitched around to face her friend. "Say, Marilyn. You haven't been sketching lately."

"I have some," Marilyn said. "Sometimes when I'm taking care of the boys, I do little sketches of them."

"But shouldn't you work at it regularly?"

"Julie, I don't have time to sketch. I have to do most of the housework now. And I'm certainly not going to give up my dates."

"But you have to give up something. You still want to be an artist, don't you?"

"Oh, I do! But I'm more sure of the dates."

"Sure of dates! Did you mention bragging?" Julie laughed.

"Stop it, Julie Brownell! You could have dates, too, if you'd quit mooning about Dave."

Julie studied her fingers as they pressed little pleats into her skirt. "Maybe I haven't mooned enough. All I've thought about is how I can be a singer. I'd do anything for lessons. Anything. Even scrub floors."

"That's not a bad idea," Marilyn said. "My mother gets eight bucks a day when she cleans."

"She does! Could she tell me where to find a job? I mean, do people ever want her where she can't go?"

"I don't know. I'll ask her." Marilyn's next words were swallowed in a yawn. "Gee! What a day!"

"Seriously, Marilyn."

"Your folks wouldn't let you."

"They will. They'll have to. Why don't you do it, too? You could earn money for art lessons."

Marilyn perked up, then drooped. "Who'd take care of the boys?"

"I'll help you. We'll manage. Won't it be super to get really started?" Julie hugged her knees and looked out over the river again, but this time with a smile. "I'll bet we're the first girls in history who've actually looked forward to scrubbing floors."

✣ 12 ✣

DAVE LAY FLAT ON HIS BACK ON THE BROWNELLS' LAWN, his eyes half closed against the glare of the sun. Seated beside him, Julie was sharply aware of his presence but paid no attention to him until she heard his sleepy drawl. "Clouds look like cotton today."

"Aren't you original!" She leaned over and tickled his nose with a long blade of grass.

Dave grabbed her wrist and pulled her toward him, but before they could start a tussle, Julie's squeal was interrupted by Marilyn. "Julie, for lands' sake, sit still!"

"Oh, sorry." Julie sat up, tucked her rumpled blouse more neatly into her shorts and resumed the set expression of a model. Beyond Marilyn she could see Mother and the youngest Hall boy at work in the garden. From the far side of the house she could hear the shouts of the older Halls, engaged in a noisy game of cowboy. Marilyn had come to sketch at least two afternoons a week all summer. "You can bring the boys and let them play in the yard," had been Julie's suggestion. "They'll be perfectly safe there, so you'll be able to work in peace."

Peace? Like a jet-propelled plane, little Eddie Hall shot
out of the garden and thrust a bouquet between Marilyn's face and her sketch pad. "Look, Mar'lyn. For Mom-
mie."

"Pretty." Marilyn pushed the flowers away, but by then
Mrs. Brownell had followed Eddie at a more leisurely pace
and stopped to ask her how she was coming.

Marilyn held her sketch at arm's length. "What do you
think?"

Mrs. Brownell glanced from the picture to her daughter,
and Julie, catching the flash of uncertainty in her expression, intercepted her reply. "It's not supposed to look just
like me, Mother. An artist interprets. Right, Marilyn?"

"Why, it's fine," Mrs. Brownell said quickly.

"Says who?" demanded Eddie and they all laughed.

Mrs. Brownell said she was going in to start the potatoes
and Julie scrambled to her feet before Dave had a chance
to help her. "I'll do it, Mother. Please. Let me," she called,
but her mother had already gone.

Marilyn scrambled too. "Is it that late? I have to go.
Eddie, call the other boys, will you?"

"Don't hurry," Julie urged, but Marilyn had to get sup-
per herself and besides, she had a date with Slim.

"I have an idea," she said. "We're going to the drive-in.
Why don't you and Dave come along?"

With Dave right behind her, Julie could only form a
frantic voiceless, "No," with her lips. Whenever Dave

came to mow the lawn, he stayed on to visit, but he had not asked for any dates and she did not want him pushed.

Marilyn was not to be silenced. "How 'bout it, Dave?"

"I dunno." Dave scuffed one foot across the grass. "It's Slim's car. He might not like it."

"Phooey! We'll pick you up around eight. 'Bye." Marilyn gathered her charges and left.

"What do you think?" Dave asked Julie. "Maybe you and I better go somewhere by ourselves."

"Whatever you say, Dave."

He rubbed his hand across the back of his neck. "I don't know Slim very well. He's older. Didn't he graduate from his school in June?"

Why, Dave's shy, too, Julie thought in surprise, and the discovery made her bolder. "I'm sure it's all right or Marilyn wouldn't have asked us."

Dave straightened up. "Okay, then. I'll beat it home and change. See you later."

"Yes. Look, I really have to help my mother." Julie hurried into the house as Dave was leaving the yard. She could not let Mother do her work, not when she had so nearly completed a summer of substituting for Sarah Lou.

As Marilyn had predicted, Julie's parents would not hear of her going out to do housework, but when Sarah Lou went to Alabama to visit her family and convalesce, they had, after three agonizing days of consideration, agreed to let Julie try her job.

"We can't pay you," Dr. Brownell had said. "Sarah Lou's salary won't stop and besides, you haven't her experience. But if you can take the heavier load off your mother's shoulders, we'll give you voice lessons in the fall."

Could she! All through one of the hottest summers on record, Julie had washed and ironed and scrubbed and cooked without complaint. In fact she often sang at her work in happy anticipation of the real job to come. And now there were only two weeks to go.

Her mother was delighted to teach her to run a house, for she hoped her daughter would eventually forget all this "singing business" and marry some nice young man. When Julie went into the kitchen with the evening's date settled, Mrs. Brownell beamed.

"I'm so pleased, Julie. You haven't had enough fun this summer, and David seems a fine boy."

"I like him." Julie dumped a bag of beans onto the table and sat down to string them. "Only sometimes I don't understand him."

"Why not?" Mother wanted to know.

"Oh, he's—changeable." Julie still wondered at the difference in Dave. After his fight with Rickie in the spring, she had been unable to reach through to him at all, but when she ran into him downtown in mid-July, he greeted her like a long-lost friend. He was a handyman this summer, he told her, and he asked if her father had any jobs he could do.

"He's always a gentleman," Mother said approvingly, "and lovely with the Hall children."

"How can he help it?" Julie chuckled. The older Hall boys all but worshipped Dave, the athlete, and often followed his lawnmower back and forth while they plied him with questions.

"He's a fine boy," Mother repeated. "I'm sure you'll have a good time tonight."

Julie had a marvelous time. As Marilyn kept saying, Slim was a panic, and he kept them all in stitches. Long before they reached the drive-in, Dave was quite relaxed and at the end of the evening, when Slim stopped his car at Julie's steps, she said, "Honestly! I've never laughed so much in my life."

"Let's do it again some time." Slim twisted around to face Dave and Julie in the back seat. "How's about Saturday night?"

"Sure, Slim," Dave agreed. "That is, if it's all right with Julie."

"I'd love it," Julie said, and Marilyn thought it would be super.

On the Saturday before Labor Day they went on their third double date. The weather, after a brief respite, had turned steamingly hot again, and for a while they just cruised around in the car to cool off. They were unusually quiet for them, their talk and laughter widely spaced and slow, but they were lazily content.

All at once Marilyn perked up. "What's that?" she asked and she pointed to where a blaze of light flared across the darkness on the road ahead.

Dave came to life next, sliding forward on his seat. "Hey! It's a miniature golf course. Let's play."

"Let's." Julie echoed his enthusiasm.

"You kids! Why can't you leave a guy in peace?" Slim grumbled, but he swerved into the parking lot so abruptly that Marilyn, bending to put her shoes back on, was nearly thrown against the windshield.

Slim reached out to catch her. "Take it easy, girl. No use to get killed before we even start."

While they sat on a bench to wait their turn, Slim kept up a running commentary of mock complaint. "Athletes! Slave drivers!" He pointed to the parking lot. "My nice comfortable car. Say, Dave, would they let you ride around this course?"

"I'll carry you," Dave offered and Slim promptly landed on his lap with a heavy plump.

By the time they started to play, they were in their usual hilarious mood, but never had it reached such heights as during their game. Dave far outshone them all, putting his ball around the man-made hazards and into the holes with amazing ease. Compared to him the girls did poorly, but Slim was simply terrible.

This did not worry Slim. The worse he played, the more he clowned. He swung his club with exaggerated movements; cajoled the ball as if it were a person; he followed its course with hand-shaded eyes, like the pictures of Columbus discovering America. After the last hole he sat right down on the ground, threw both arms over his head and shook with spurious sobs.

Slim had roused them all from their lethargy and it was a merry foursome that bounced into Jo Jo's a half hour later. Nor did he let up then. He teased the waitress until, helpless with laughter, she laid her pad on the table and said, "Here. You write the order."

Julie noticed with a touch of pride that she put the pad in front of Dave. Much as she liked and enjoyed Slim's antics, she could not help but be glad that the more dignified Dave was her date.

They had scarcely taken the first taste of their banana splits when Anna Jensen came through the door with a boy from the basketball team. Julie had been seeing Anna off and on all summer and knew that she had broken off with Louis, but she had not heard about this new date. Partly because they were all in a boisterous mood and partly through surprise, she spoke louder than she intended.

"There's Anna Jensen with Johnny Trent!"

At the sound of her name Anna turned, and when she caught sight of Julie, came toward her with Johnny close behind.

"Hi, Julie. Marilyn. Dave." She glanced uncertainly at Slim till Julie introduced them

Slim rose to acknowledge the introduction but Dave remained seated. Unlike Marilyn's friendly, "Hi," his greeting to Anna had been hardly more than a grunt and he was even less cordial to Johnny.

Anna failed to notice. "Can't we all sit together?" she bubbled. "We could pull up a couple of chairs, couldn't we, Johnny?"

"Sure." As Johnny went off to get the chairs, Julie nudged Dave in the hope that he would help, but he only became more rigid. The high spirits of the others had been quenched too. Marilyn and Slim continued to be polite but the gaiety was gone. Julie struggled to make conversation, while her ice cream melted and Dave sulked at her side. At last Slim asked her if she had finished and suggested that they leave.

He and Dave both reached for the check. Their fingers closed over it simultaneously and Dave withdrew his hand without protest. Did he have to make himself look like a cheapskate in front of Anna? Always before, he had insisted on paying for the refreshments, since Slim bore the expense of the car.

They drove home in an atmosphere of constraint. In the front seat Marilyn and Slim talked idly but Dave maintained his resentful silence while Julie seethed. When the car came to her stairway, she boiled over.

"You don't have to wait for Dave," she told Slim. "He's going to stay here for a while."

Dave stopped with one foot on the ground and the other still in the car. "What's the big idea?"

Amazed at her own temerity, Julie gave him a little push. "Good night, Marilyn. 'Night, Slim. Thanks a lot."

Slim hesitated, scratching at his cheek, until Marilyn said, "Let's go, Slim. Can't you see they want to be alone?"

Marilyn's implication momentarily took the wind out of Julie's sails, and it was not until Slim's tail lights had disappeared into the darkness that she turned on Dave. "Did you have to be rude to my friends?"

Dave jabbed his hands into his pockets. "I told you not to mix me with those people."

"I didn't mix you. They came in. They were friendly. And how did you act?"

"Listen, Julie Brownell. If you think I'm going to let them patronize me, you're all wrong. I thought you'd be different away from school, but no. Even in summer you beg for their smug condescension."

"Anna Jensen does not condescend!"

"You and your Anna! I once thought a friend would always be loyal, but I found out different. You will too. Wait and see."

"I already have. I've also found out that you can't judge the whole world by one person. Like—like Rickie Sheridan."

"You shut up!" Dave grabbed Julie's arm in a painful grip but immediately relaxed his grasp. "I'm sorry, Julie."

"It's all right." Dave's sudden meekness deflated her.

She leaned against the pillar at the foot of the steps, and its stones, still warm from the sun, dug roughly into her back.

Dave said, "I'd better shove off."

Julie stepped toward him. "Dave, please don't try to make me choose between you and Anna."

"It's none of my business." Dave shrugged. "You do whatever you like."

"I don't know, Dave." Julie sank onto the steps. "My father thinks we ought to try and make friends. It's not always easy, but it works, at least with some people."

"I don't want their friendship," Dave flared.

"But you need it. How're you going to play basketball if you're mad at everyone on the team?"

"That's easy," Dave said. "I'm quitting basketball."

"You can't do that!" Julie jumped up to face him. "It's your main asset around school. It's part of you. If you quit, you won't be yourself any more."

"Who cares?"

"I do," said Julie in a small voice.

Dave's scowl melted into startled surprise. He shook his head as if to clear it of a mirage. "Come on, Julie," he said gently. "This isn't getting us anywhere." He took her arm and they started up the stairs.

Julie did not speak again until they reached the first landing. "Maybe it will be better this year."

"What will?"

"Basketball."

"Oh, that." Dave sounded indifferent.

Julie dared not mention Rickie again, could not say that since he had dropped Bets, he might return to Dave. Anyway, what if he did? Wouldn't it be too late, as it had been for Doris and herself?

Dave broke into her thoughts. "Maybe you're right. I guess I would be pretty miserable without athletics."

"You'll try it then?" Julie asked.

"I'll see, Julie. I'll see."

Julie could argue no more. Despite Lorraine, despite the still unsettled George, she had mostly considered this problem as a personal one. But now she could see that there were others who faced it; especially there was Dave. No definite thought formed in her mind, no picture of thousands of dark faces came before her eyes, but she felt an inexplicable burden on her shoulders, a burden she did not want to bear. It had been a long evening and she was exhausted. Gratefully she leaned against the strength of Dave's arm, and together they climbed to the top of the stairs.

🙙 13 🙜

JULIE SAT IN THE CAR BESIDE HER FATHER, LOOKING straight ahead. Excitement formed a tight knot in the pit of her stomach, but she kept her hands relaxed in her lap. This was no time to get nervous. It was the most important day in her life so far, for she was on her way to apply to Signora Petrucelli for voice lessons.

Signora Petrucelli was, without question, the best voice teacher in town. A former prima donna, she was reputed to be an eccentric, devoted to music and cats, and very choosy about her pupils. Serious intent and talent were not always enough for her. She had been known to refuse a pupil on a whim. Julie's triumph at being granted an audition had been diluted by the curt words, "This does not mean I shall accept you."

Remembering, she said, "At least I have a chance."

"A good chance," Daddy assured her. "But don't feel too disappointed if she turns you down. There are other good teachers."

"Not as good as Petrucelli." Ever so slightly Julie's fingers tightened and twisted. She could not wholly forget the way her voice had wavered at the church dinner, nor obliterate the memory of that other teacher, concerned for those of her pupils who might resent a girl not like themselves. Something like that could finish the whole project for Daddy. Julie had begged him not to come with her, but he thought a teacher would want assurance that a young girl had the financial backing of her parents.

Daddy noticed her tension. "Try to relax. Take deep breaths," he advised.

"Okay." Julie breathed deeply over and over as they sped through traffic, and managed to keep it up during her father's interminable maneuvers to wedge between two cars on the crowded apartment-lined street which was their destination. In the creaky apartment elevator she purposely let her arms and shoulders fall limp, but when Signora Petrucelli opened her door to them, she snapped alert, searching the sharp brown eyes for a sign of acceptance or rejection.

Dr. Brownell explained who they were.

"Oh, yes." Signora Petrucelli stroked the yellow cat held against her ample bosom. "The girl Ruth Adams recommended."

"That's right," Julie said eagerly. There had been no evasion in those glittering eyes, no surprise on the sallow, wrinkled face.

"Don't think I take advice. Not from Ruth Adams or anyone else." The Signora's head of frowzy iron-gray hair bobbed emphatically, but she stepped aside to let them in.

Julie had never seen such a cluttered room. The mantel over the tiled fireplace held an unbelievable collection of vases, pictures and knickknacks; shelves lining the walls were piled with books, magazines, frayed sheet music, several hats and a molted fur piece. The dusty leaves of a rubber plant were etched against the yellowed coarse lace curtains at the windows, and countless ferns stood on small tables crowded among the chairs and ornate lamps. Only the grand piano was clear of debris, but beneath it a fat mother cat was washing a family of kittens.

Signora Petrucelli sent Dr. Brownell into exile. "We shall not need an audience. You may wait in the kitchen."

"Certainly." Dr. Brownell sounded almost meek, but Julie was reassured by the twinkle behind his smile.

"Now." With another jerk of her head, Signora Petrucelli summoned Julie to the piano and slid onto the bench, setting the yellow cat beside her. Her hands ran lightly over the keyboard while she studied Julie with a penetrating stare. "So you want to sing."

"I want to learn." Julie laid her music on the piano and pressed her knees together to stop their quaking.

"Learn! You must have the voice. You must work and work and work."

"I know." Alarmed that even her speaking voice was thin with fright, Julie tried another deep breath.

Without warning, Signora Petrucelli struck a middle-C chord. "A-a-ah," she instructed.

Julie took one more breath and sang, "A-a-ah." The

quiver was not pronounced, but heavens! where was her power? She ran up the chromatic scale, straining for volume, but the higher the note, the weaker her tones became.

"Contralto," the Signora muttered, and she dropped back to middle C and played downward. This was better. But Julie had hardly reached her stride when the music teacher stopped her.

"How's your reading?" she snapped, and without waiting for an answer, miraculously found the very piece of music she wanted from the jumbled shelf at her side and thrust it into Julie's hands. "Know this?"

Julie opened the music and saw that it was a Welsh folk song. "No," she said. "I haven't seen it before."

"Try it."

As she listened to the introduction and started to sing, Julie was unaware that she beat one foot to the rhythm. Not so the kittens under the piano. Attracted by the movement, two of them pounced on her ankle and her third note ended in a screech.

Signora Petrucelli snatched her hands from the keyboard and looked at Julie with disapproval. "You're not afraid of cats!"

"N-no." Julie could still feel the prick of sharp little claws. "They startled me. That's all."

"My girl, you must never let anything distract you. Once, in Rome, my feathered headdress fell across my face, but I did not lose a note. Just tore it off and went on singing."

Ordinarily the picture of this ramrod woman with feathers drooping over her face would have made Julie laugh. But now she had to concentrate on singing while two kittens rolled over her feet and the yellow cat seemed ready to spring at any moment. Definitely not at her best, she was dismayed when the Signora cut her off.

"That's enough. Now let me hear something you know."

Julie's mind went blank, but only for a second. " 'He—he shall feed his flock?' " she asked.

"Very well." Signora Petrucelli reached for the music and propped it against the rack. She began to play; the cat switched its tail; Julie sang.

She looked away from the Signora toward a mirror which hung on the wall. As she sang, she watched her reflection but did not really see it because all her thoughts were with her music. This time the Signora let her sing it through.

It had not gone badly. Julie turned back to the piano, her eyes wide with unspoken questions. Had it been good enough? Had it offset the weak scales and shaky folk song? The Signora's expression was noncommittal and all she said was, "Get me your father."

Daddy was in the kitchen playing with yet another cat, a striped one. The tabby followed him into the living room, constantly tangling with his legs as he picked his way through the furniture. By this time the yellow cat was jumping on the piano keys, and his mistress had to yell to make herself heard.

"Your daughter shows some promise, Dr. Brownell. I cannot say how she'll develop, but I am willing to give her a try."

I've made it! Julie clapped her hand over her mouth to keep from shouting. She hardly heard the rest of the conversation nor the feline cacophony which filled the room. She had been accepted by the great Petrucelli! Nothing could stop her now.

She was not in the least daunted by the Signora's final warning. "Remember this is only a trial. You young people are apt to dissipate your energies, but my pupils must think of music, music, nothing but music."

"I will!" Julie promised. "I will!"

All the way home she babbled happily, giggling at the ups and downs of her tryout, dreaming aloud of her glorious future. Juilliard, her own concerts, maybe even the Metropolitan Opera. One last dream she kept to herself, the vision of the Julie to come, sought after, fussed over, welcome everywhere.

Daddy seemed as pleased as she was, and he paid her a compliment too. "You've grown up a lot, Julie. Two years ago Signora Petrucelli would have floored you."

"Don't think I wasn't scared," Julie admitted. "But I did get through it, didn't I? So now do you believe I have the temperament?"

"I think you can develop it," Daddy conceded. "I wish you hadn't chosen such a hard life, but you do have talent. I hope you'll use it well."

"Daddy! You don't have to tell me to work."

"That's not what I meant," he said. "If you're a success, doors which are closed to many of us may be opened to you. Always remember to hold the door wide so that others may come in."

Julie's eyes darted toward her father and back to the road ahead. Yes, but what of those who would not come in, people who followed the line of least resistance, like Marilyn, or rebelled openly, like Dave?

"You can't make people be friendly," she argued.

"You can try."

But she had already tried and failed. Marilyn would not budge from her narrow circle. Dave's friendliness in the week since she had urged him toward athletics had been no more than casual. Perhaps she had not tried hard enough, had been a fair-weather friend to Dave. If only she could make him like her a lot, she might be able to pull him through the door.

Quite suddenly her mind switched back to the day's success. Happiness flooded over her and with it a confidence which encompassed her whole world. Anything seemed possible. How could she miss with Dave?

"You don't need to worry, Daddy," she said. "From now on, everything's going to be fine."

⚹ 14 ⚹

JULIE LEANED OVER THE EDGE OF THE BALCONY AND HER hands gripped its iron rail. A cold March wind blew through the open windows of the gym, but she felt no need of the coat that lay rumpled in the chair behind her. She might have been down there on the court herself, so closely did she follow Dave's movements.

There. He had the ball now. He and a shadowing guard tore down the court, feet stamping, ball slapping against the wood of the floor. Don't shoot, Dave. Send it to Rickie. Dave, no! He had tried a long shot. The ball teetered on the rim of the basket. Make it go in, Julie willed, and to her surprise, it did.

"We're ahead!" Marilyn shrieked and the whistle blew to end the game. Everyone else jumped up, yelling, but Julie sank back into her seat with a happy sigh. Tonight, in the last game of the season, Dave had been at his brilliant best.

It had not always been this way. In many of the games he had fouled out early or muffed shots and been taken out. Then would come a night like this when he would return to his old form, the lightning speed, the accuracy, the quickness of judgment.

"Funny thing," he once told Julie. "I always play best just when I've decided the heck with it."

"Maybe you're trying too hard, Dave. I mean, that's what Signora Petrucelli sometimes says about me."

The teams were leaving the gym and Slim leaned behind Marilyn's shoulders to rouse Julie. "Whassa matter? Don't you know your boy's a hero?"

"Really?" Julie bent forward and saw that this time Dave walked in the midst of the other fellows. Could it be that tonight's success had wiped out the last of his hostility? She knew it had been lessening as his relationship with his teammates had grown continually less formal and polite, but he had never quite reached the point of complete trust.

Marilyn turned around and rested back against the rail. "Julie, can't you get Dave to stay for the dancing?"

"Aw, what for?" Slim interrupted. A man of the world now, he did not particularly care for school affairs and had only come to the game for Marilyn's sake.

"Please," Marilyn begged, and Slim threw out his arms in a gesture of helplessness.

"What can you do with a woman like that?"

Marilyn followed up her victory quickly, reaching to pull Julie to her feet. "Let's go fix ourselves up."

"I don't think Dave will stay," Julie protested as they started off.

"So then we'll go out somewhere like we planned."

Marilyn stepped closer to Julie and lowered her voice. "Guess who I saw today?"

"Who?"

"Your cousin George. He drove me home in the swankiest red convertible I ever saw. He must be in the money."

"Mm." Julie could not tell Marilyn that the latest of George's many jobs was not quite on the level. "How come you're riding around with George? I thought you were going steady with Slim."

"Ya, but that doesn't mean I can't ever ride with another fellow. 'Specially in a car like that."

"You're just a gold digger," Jule said, laughing.

They found the washroom packed, and it was some time before they got back to Slim at the gym's door.

"Where you been? Australia?" he complained. "Orchestra's been playin' for about a week."

"You two go in and dance," Julie said. "I'll wait for Dave."

But how could she persuade him to stay for the dance, when he had steadily refused to enter into any school activities except athletics? He would not even try out for *High Button Shoes*, the musical comedy for which rehearsals were to start next week.

"But everyone's going to be in it," Julie had said.

"Not Marilyn, I bet."

"You know very well she can't, not when she works afternoons."

"The answer is still no, Julie. I don't go for this school stuff."

Julie had said no more, fearing a repetition of last autumn. How often they had argued about his refusal to go out for fall track! Sometimes he had brought the subject up himself, thinking aloud as he tried to figure out what he ought to do. But whenever he came close to her in this way, he would withdraw and avoid her for days at a time.

It had been Signora Petrucelli, indirectly, who had pushed Dave into basketball. The music teacher was a hard taskmaster, very hard. She criticized and tore down until there were times when Julie felt she could not go on.

One night after a particularly tough lesson, Dave took Julie bowling. He had taught her to bowl and usually they had many a laugh over her awkwardness with the big ball. But that night nothing seemed funny to Julie nor could she pull herself out of her black mood. When, over hamburgers, Dave asked what was the matter, she spilled out all her troubles.

Dave's face clouded. "It's that teacher, Julie. Why don't you take lessons from someone else? Our choir director, for instance?"

Though she had considered a change of teacher herself, Julie was shocked when the words were spoken aloud. "But she's the best teacher in town. In the whole county, I guess."

"Not for you, she isn't. She'll never give you a break because you're not her kind."

"Then why did she take me?" An edge of stridency crept into Julie's voice. "She doesn't take everybody."

Dave shrugged. "Maybe to get your money. Maybe to make herself look broadminded."

Julie rose to her music teacher's defense. "She's not like that at all."

"They all are, Julie. Even your friend Anna. That's why I don't want any part of them."

Anna again. Julie bristled. "That's not why, and you know it. You won't give Anna a chance because you're afraid. You're a coward, that's what."

Appalled at what she had said, Julie gaped at Dave's furious scowl, saw his knuckles tighten over the edge of the table. Timidly she reached toward those knuckles. "I'm sorry, Dave. I didn't mean it."

Dave snatched his hand away, and his words pierced like sharp little icicles. "If you've finished, let's go."

Another silent trip home while Julie berated herself. Why couldn't she be like Marilyn, able to twist any fellow around her little finger? Why had she let herself use sledge-hammer methods?

To her amazement, her violence did more than all her gentle persuasion. Two days later Dave came to her, apologetic and rather sheepish. "I've decided you're right, Julie. And if you can take it, so can I. I'm going out for basketball."

Well, she did not want to try the same method again. Besides, she could no longer use herself as an example.

She was getting along better with the Signora, had even drummed up courage to ask her permission to take part in the musical comedy. Still a bit afraid of the music teacher, knowing she was against the overtaxing of a young voice, Julie had broached the subject cautiously. She could still hear the boom of the Signora's reply. "The lead?"

"Oh, no." Julie had her eyes on the future now and was content to wait.

"You might be in the chorus," Signora Petrucelli conceded. "The stage experience will be good for you. But no solos, not yet. And don't use your full voice at rehearsals."

Julie had made the chorus easily. It had hurt a little to have to give up the chance for a solo, especially when Bets Hampton had one of the lead parts—Bets, who could not really sing a note. But at least she was in it and she was making progress with her voice lessons and Dave was her constant attendant. If only he would be in the musical comedy, life would be perfect.

Hey! Where was the fellow? Julie shook herself from her memories and saw Rickie Sheridan and some of the other members of the squad coming from the direction of the locker room.

Rickie raised one hand in salute. "Dave'll be along in a minute."

"Thanks, Rickie. Good game," Julie said.

Rickie had been very friendly lately. Sometimes she wondered if he was trying to win back Dave through her. She could not forgive him for hurting Dave, but he must have some good in him. Anna Jensen would never rave so over a phony.

There was Dave now, not alone but with Johnny Trent. Johnny's pounding fists and the shake of Dave's head indicated an argument, but neither boy seemed angry. When they reached Julie, Johnny said, "How do you stand this guy? Most stubborn character I've ever met."

"You get used to it." Julie smiled at Johnny and then at Dave.

"No, I mean it," Johnny insisted. "They want the squad for a comedy dance in *High Button Shoes,* but do you think Dave'll come along? Nothing doing."

Dave ran his hand over his hair. "I'm no dancer."

"Who is?" Johnny demanded.

Julie said, "You fellows played a wonderful game."

"Ya, we're hot stuff," Johnny agreed amiably. "Wait'll you see us as ballerinas." He nodded toward the gym. "You two coming in?"

Julie waited for Dave to answer.

"I dunno," he said. "We sort of have a date with another couple."

"Aw, you're just plain antisocial." Johnny brushed them off with a gesture of his hand. "See you," he said, and he walked on.

"Marilyn and Slim are in dancing," Julie told Dave.

"Yeah? Slim?" Dave's eyebrows shot up. "Well, I suppose we might as well try it for a while."

Julie could hardly curb an astonished, "What!" and

there were so many people milling around that she did not really have a chance to talk to Dave until they had started to dance.

"You were terrific tonight," she said.

"Think so?" Dave sounded confident. "I wasn't sure about that last shot. It should have gone to Rickie but I was afraid there wasn't time."

"But you made it. You practically won the game."

"That's what the fellows said." Dave steered Julie around a pair of jitterbugs. "You know they've been pretty decent this year. Even when my game was lousy."

"Then why don't you want to be in the ballet?"

"Should I?"

"Of course, stupid. Don't you ever listen when I talk?"

"Nope. You talk too much." Dave dropped his arm from Julie's waist but still held one of her hands. "Okay, swing it, girl," he said. "If I'm going to be a ballet dancer, I'd better get in form."

The first weeks of rehearsal were like one big party. Though different parts of the cast practiced in different rooms, they often stole in to watch one another or went in crowds to The Hangout. Thrown with Anna through Julie, Dave gradually succumbed to her natural friendliness, and as the days went by, neither he nor Julie gave a thought to being the only Negroes in the cast.

The comedy dance number was funnier than the choreography warranted. The boys, so graceful on a basketball court, were all arms and legs and awkwardness as they took wrong turns and stumbled over one another's feet. Even the teacher-director was amused.

About ten days before the performance, a new spirit crept into the cast. The fun was over as they knuckled down to serious work; outbursts of temperament were common among both students and teachers; last-minute fittings were accompanied by groans, as carefully made costumes fell short of the mark.

In a way Julie liked this part best of all, for with the tension was excitement, concentration and eager anticipation. This was theater, the life she had chosen, and the future stretched before her in a glorious panorama.

It was at one of these last rehearsals that Bev Blake climbed onto a chair and clapped for attention. "Listen, everybody," she called out. "I'm having a party at the country club after the Saturday night show. You're all invited."

"Think we ought to go?" Dave asked Julie afterward.

"Why not? She invited all of us, didn't she?"

"Yes, but you know. The country club and all."

"Don't you want to go?"

"Well—if you think it's all right."

"Of course it is, Dave. It's a school party, isn't it?"

On Saturday night Julie packed her pale-blue taffeta in a box and started out in a frenzy of excitement. The Friday performance had gone well and now there was one more chance to sing on stage, and then the country club.

She had never been to a school party, and it was a wish come true.

A bigger audience made the second performance an even more stimulating experience than the first. In the dressing room afterward, pleased with themselves and released from nervous tension, the girls giggled and capered and squealed like small children just out of school. Julie, pulling her dress over her head, was nearly knocked off her feet as someone dashed by. She fell against Evvy Newton, who roared in mock dismay.

"Do you have to hog the whole mirror?" Anna pushed in beside Julie. "How're you getting there? To the country club, I mean."

"Dave has his father's car. Want to come with us?"

"Love to." Anna, applying lipstick, mumbled through tightened lips. "It's all right to play the field, but sometimes you get stuck without a date. Like me, tonight."

The car was already filled with fellows but Anna managed to squeeze in. It was a hilarious trip. Dave, who had never been to the country club, lost his way and the boys ribbed him unmercifully. In their crazy mood, even the most commonplace remark brought shrieks of laughter. When they finally reached their destination, Julie got out of the car and hugged her sides. "Whew! I'm exhausted already."

She was not really tired and practically skipped through the wide doors of the country club into the spacious, brightly lighted hall. Most of the others were already there, shifting around behind Bev and her parents, who stood near the entrance to receive their guests. The sound of distant music formed a soft background to the excited chatter in the room.

It's like a scene from a movie, Julie thought, feeling the soft carpet under her feet, entranced by the glitter of glass chandeliers, the girls in gay formals and the boys slicked up to unrecognizable splendor.

"Might as well get in line." Anna smiled at Johnny Trent, who obliged by joining her. Julie and Dave stepped up behind them and watched Bev's tall, distinguished father as he welcomed the others to the party.

"We're next," Julie whispered and Mr. Blake turned toward her, extending his hand. She felt it close over hers, but there had been no mistaking its momentary hesitation nor the startled expression which preceded his "Good evening."

Julie was jabbed by a prick of foreboding, but she said, "Good evening," and introduced Dave and herself.

Mr. Blake turned to his daughter, but Bev was talking to Anna, nor could he get the attention of his wife. He looked at Julie and Dave again. "I don't know what to say. Beverly didn't tell us . . ."

Julie's panic spread. Though she neither glanced at Dave nor touched him, she could feel his fury rising, steely cold. What shall I do, she thought wildly, but Bev's voice brought temporary calm.

"Daddy, this is Julie Brownell and David Ross."

"Beverly, my dear . . ." Mr. Blake pulled out his handkerchief and wiped his forehead. Once more he cast a look of appeal at his wife, and this time she caught his signal.

Her eyes flicked from him to Julie and Dave, and back to him. "Robert. Go speak to the manager. Maybe he'll let us make an exception." She smiled too brightly at the two young Negroes, nodding her head in quick little jiggles.

"What's the matter?" Bev's shrillness silenced the crowd so that though Dave spoke quietly enough, his voice resounded through the room. "Come on, Julie. We aren't wanted here."

For a lifelong second, Julie stood numb. The faces before her blurred into a flesh-colored mass. One pink blob emerged and came toward her, but she had barely recognized it as Anna's face before Dave snatched her arm and pulled her across the hall. They walked through the door and it closed behind them.

"Friends!" Dave snarled. "Make friends. Well, now you know what friends mean."

Julie, still numb, only stared.

"I won't forget this, Julie. Not ever. I'll get back at them if it's the last thing I do." Dave clenched his fists and glared at the building.

A shaking started in Julie's knees and spread up through her body. What could she say? She, too, stood in the shadows beyond the light which poured through the windows; she, too, heard the music and voices muted by the brick of impenetrable walls. Confused, almost unable to grasp what had happened, she automatically spoke the words she had heard so often. "Hate won't help, Dave."

"Oh, no? We'll see. You can go on licking their boots, but I'll fight back with everything I've got."

Julie shivered and shook in the warm night, and Dave, noticing, relented. "You're cold!" He put his arm around her shoulders. "Let's get out of here," he said and he led her to the car.

As he jerked out of his parking space, Julie heard the crash of fender against fender. She opened her mouth to scream but no sound came. Her hand flew to her neck and she felt her vocal cords, taut and unresponsive. Well, it didn't matter. It didn't matter at all. She would never sing again.

✌ 15 ✌

For Julie, nothing had ever been as hard as returning to school on Monday. That first day back in her freshman year had been bad enough, but then her hurt had been private; then she had not been disgraced before all her friends.

But she had to go, could not afford to skip school, not with Juilliard as her goal. Her resolve never to sing again had not lasted twenty-four hours, and Sunday afternoon had found her back at the piano, practicing conscientiously if without zest. Her dream had faded, but music had become a part of her and she could no more do without singing than food.

"Daddy, why don't you drive Julie to school today?" Mother suggested at breakfast.

"Would you?" Julie faced her father. They could start early and she could dash into the building and be hidden behind her books by the time the others arrived.

"Of course, if you want me to," Daddy said. "Only won't you feel better if you see this through by yourself?"

Julie was pulled in two directions; toward her mother, inarticulate, who had shown her sympathy by pampering;

toward her father who, even in compassion, had held her to courageous acceptance. She slumped over her plate.

"Daddy's right. I'll go alone."

She started out on feet which seemed detached from her body, for though her tread was firm, she quaked inwardly. As she approached the Regans' she saw Doris come out of the house and involuntarily waved. Doris had not been at the party, would not know what had happened.

But Doris knew. "I heard about Saturday night, Julie. Gee! That was awful."

"It doesn't matter," Julie said.

"But I don't understand it," Doris persisted. "You're so popular and all."

You understood once, Julie thought bitterly, but again she said, "It really doesn't matter."

Bev Blake met her at the school gate, gushing with a remorse which broke down the careful manner she usually used with Julie. It was embarrassing and it was a relief when Bets Hampton came along and snatched Bev away, reminding her of the homework they had to finish before school. As they walked off, Bets spoke loudly enough for Julie to hear.

"Don't worry so, Bev. She should have known better than to go there."

In the whole school, only Bets was inexorable. Everyone else was sympathetic; Anna and Evvy and all Julie's friends, other girls whom she knew only slightly, boys who had never talked with her before. Julie accepted their commiseration graciously but with aching heart. It was only another way of setting her apart.

And it kept her from Dave. Twice he approached her, once in the schoolyard and once in the corridor, but when he saw her surrounded, hurried off before she could reach him. She had never wanted him so much, yet was half afraid to see him. No one could have been more gentle than he on Saturday night, concerned about her chill, rushing her to a diner to warm herself with a cup of hot chocolate. They ordered food, too, but neither could eat. Both sat in the dreary diner with memories of the gay scene they had been allowed to glimpse so briefly.

Dave's anger, personal at first, had gradually spread to her behalf. It had given her a sense of protection, still when he had leaned across the table, urgent, serious, when he had said, "Don't you see we have to fight?" she could only reply with a twist of her head. Her philosophy, though shaken, was too firmly embedded to be abandoned quickly.

All morning her efforts to get to Dave were futile and she had no classes with him until after lunch. Toward noon, Johnny Trent stopped her in the hall.

"Julie, I feel terrible about the other night. I'm responsible, sort of, because I talked Dave into it."

Julie fell back on her usual, "It doesn't matter."

"It does matter!" Johnny said. "Gosh! Having your girl insulted that way! I tried to talk to Dave, but you can't get near the guy with a ten-foot pole."

"Oh." So that's how Dave was acting.

"We're all for him, Julie. For you too. Only every once in a while he gets up on his high horse this way—well, tell him, will you?"

"I'll tell him," Julie said, but she knew it would be useless.

The first period of the afternoon came at last. When Julie entered the room, Dave was slouched in his seat glowering into space, nor could she make him look in her direction. She waited for him after class and fell in beside him. "Where you been all day?"

"Around." Dave glanced down at her. "You seem to be doing all right."

"You could too, if you wanted to."

"Don't worry about me. I'm fine."

"Dave, they're trying to be nice. They're truly sorry."

"Yeah! Do you think for one minute that it wouldn't happen again?"

She was saved from answering by Rickie Sheridan, who came along the hall from the opposite direction and stepped out to speak to them.

Dave yanked Julie away. "That's one place I draw the line. Believe me, Julie, he'll only hurt you."

Though disconcerted about Rickie, Julie was warmed once more by Dave's protectiveness. But his next words shattered her.

"He won't hurt me, though. No one will. From now on they'll treat me right, or else!" He touched Julie's shoulder. "S'long, now," he said, and he started toward the stairs.

Julie stood where she was, paralyzed with horror. Dave had sounded just like George!

Please, please don't let him get that way! The half-prayer filled her mind so that when she was called upon in math, she did not hear what was asked. She rose, hot-faced and stammering, but the teacher, usually sharply sarcastic, merely repeated the question. In still another way, Julie had been set apart.

She moved through the week in strange detachment. Everyone was nice to her, too nice. Girls who had been relaxed and easy unconsciously adopted the meticulous manner of Beverly Blake. Or there would be an uncomfortable pause when someone would accidentally start to talk about the party, only to be nudged to blushing silence.

Julie understood their restraint. The incident at the country club had drawn a curtain between them which neither she nor they knew how to penetrate. She could not reject their well-meant kindness but felt imprisoned by it. Could Dave be right, or Marilyn? Was it better, after all, to give up and withdraw, either in bitterness or pretended indifference?

The tug between Dave and her white friends, the specialized treatment made her nervous and tense, and this crept into her singing. Desperately she struggled to release her voice, but the harder she tried, the more it tightened, and on Friday she went to her lesson with dread.

The lesson did go poorly but, incredibly, Signora Petrucelli was patient, limiting her censure to an occasional scowl or an, "Again, Julie. Try it again." Then, abruptly, she closed the piano. A quick look at the clock confirmed Julie's suspicion that she had not been given her full half hour and she steeled herself for the inevitable tirade.

Signora Petrucelli ran her hand through her unkempt hair. "You'd have to know some time, Julie. People are fickle."

"People?" Julie did not understand.

The Signora nodded. "One minute they flatter and fawn, but they're all too ready to forget, even to turn against you. It only takes one or two. The rest follow like stupid sheep."

So word of her humiliation had traveled all the way to this apartment. With one finger Julie traced a pattern on the piano top, not knowing what to say.

Signora Petrucelli rose and straightened her music. "I can teach you to sing, but the rest, no. You must yourself learn to keep the troubles from your voice."

"I'll try, Signora. I really will."

"Yes." The Signora's head bobbed. "I have something for you, Julie. Come along."

Julie followed her teacher to the kitchen. On the cluttered table was a hatbox punched with holes and partly filled with shredded paper. Signora Petrucelli stepped to the corner where a new family of kittens squirmed in a furry mass. She picked up a black one with a white nose and handed it to Julie. "Name's Verdi."

"For me?" Julie held the kitten at arms' length, her experience at her tryout having turned her against the entire feline world. Verdi wriggled till she nearly dropped him.

"He has to get used to you." Signora Petrucelli put the kitten into the box and clapped on the lid. "Now hurry home, Julie. He won't like it in here at all."

"Th-thank you. Thank you very much." The last thing Julie wanted was a kitten, but she was touched by her teacher's thought.

She carried the box by the string. Verdi's movements made it seesaw precariously, so she put both arms around it and held her music pressed between the box and her chest. It continued to teeter until the music slipped out and fluttered to the ground. Julie bent to retrieve it and her pocketbook slipped from her wrist and followed the music, its contents scattering over the sidewalk.

There was nothing to do but set the box down. As she scrambled to collect her possessions, the giggles of two small boys made her twist toward them. When she saw the box jerking along the curb as if by its own momentum, Julie laughed, too, really laughed for the first time in a week.

On the bus Verdi began to howl with all the power of his little cat lungs. The other passengers turned to see what was up, some with snickers, others with annoyance. Embarrassed, Julie took the kitten out of the box. It struggled to free itself, scratching at her wrists, but she tried to cuddle it and talked to it softly as she had so often seen Signora Petrucelli do.

Verdi succumbed at last and curled up in her lap, purring with contentment. Julie laid her hand on his soft, warm body and was surprised by a sudden welling of affection, not only for the kitten but for the Signora who had met her need with her choicest gift, for all those girls who had done their best to help her over a hard spot. No, withdrawal was not the way. If only Dave could understand!

❧ 16 ❧

ON AN EVENING IN APRIL, TWO YOUNG NEGROES WERE turned away from a party at the Valley View Country Club. Not a week later, hundreds of boys and girls at Hadley High had become acutely aware of social injustice, had begun to examine their own attitudes and practices.

No one talked about it, at least not to Julie, but she was aware of the change. Elise Atkins reported in wonderment that at least thirty people had urged her to attend the junior picnic. Among the seniors, a Negro boy was chosen to present the class gift at commencement, a boy hitherto as much an unknown as Doris Regan. Practically everyone in the sketch club made a point of asking Marilyn to join again.

The colored students reacted in various ways. Elise, not wholly credulous, was none the less pleased. "Don't know what the idea is," she said, "but it makes you feel kind of good."

Marilyn was cynical, sure that once she was back in the sketch club, they would bunch up and forget her as they

had before. Still, she considered ways of rearranging her
schedule to fit it in, thinking that the added instruction
from the teacher-sponsor might help her to get a job in art
when she finished school.

Dave reported that the senior boy was knocking himself
out on his presentation speech, "the sucker!"

Julie was confused by her own feelings about the new
trend. Over and over she told herself it was good, that it
had brought a smile to Elise's face, hope to Marilyn and
honor to the senior boy. But it also denied individuality,
lumped them all into an undifferentiated mass.

"It's as if we were a bunch of invalids," she complained
to Dave, "and couldn't get around by ourselves."

They were sitting on an embankment over the river
where they had stopped to rest in the midst of a Sunday
walk. Dave pulled up a clump of grass, tossed it away.
"Why take it? I don't."

Julie was impressed by the calmness of his tone, by a
composure she had not detected before. In making himself a potential powder keg, Dave had escaped the over-
whelming sponsorship and gained an independence which
seemed to give him strength. But didn't this invite further
discrimination, make it that much harder for the others?
Julie felt an unwelcome stab of obligation and cried out
against it.

"I don't want to be a—a race. I just want to be a girl."

"There's a way. I have it figured." Dave moved to put
an arm around her and pointed to the river where all sorts

of small yachts were out in Sunday profusion. "See those boats?"

Julie nodded, squinting against the sun-bright waves.

"Some day I'll have one, the biggest on the river. I'll have the fastest car too. Power! That's the answer. And when I have it, I'll show them all."

Though still controlled, Dave was impassioned and his vehemence called up an old echo to Julie's ears. *They're afraid of me because I'm tough.*

"It doesn't work!" she protested and she told Dave about George. "He must have had fifteen jobs in the past two years. Last time he was a numbers runner, but he quit that too. He wasn't even satisfied to break the law."

"You don't need to worry about me," Dave assured her. "I'll work. I'll work because my plans take money. Plenty of it."

He had already begun to look for a summer job, but so had many of his classmates, and there were more applicants than vacancies. Daily he went to the school office where employment opportunities were listed, but was always told there was nothing suitable for him. His resentment seethed and Julie, hoping to help prevent an outburst, secretly watched the newspaper ads in his behalf.

Every day someone came to school with news of success. Johnny Trent landed a counsellor job at the camp to which he had gone as a younger boy. A family in Anna's church asked her to spend the summer with them at the shore, to help take care of their children. Through the influence of his father, Rickie Sheridan found a spot in a New York office. Marilyn would go on full time at the laundry in which she had been working afternoons.

"I could get Dave a job there," she told Julie. "But I suppose he's too darn proud."

Yes, Dave was proud and Julie was proud of his pride. She recognized the gallantry in Marilyn's cheerful acceptance of a bad lot, but how often Marilyn lost sight of her goal!

Not Dave. With dogged determination he pursued his purpose, tapping every resource. He finally went so far as to gulp down that fierce pride and accept an offer of help from a white man, a lawyer who was a prominent member of the church where his father was sexton. It was this lawyer, Mr. Halliday, who arranged an interview with the personnel manager of a local firm.

Dave came to school that morning, excited, and dressed in his Sunday best, light-gray suit, white shirt, deep-red tie. After dismissal, Julie walked to the gate with him to give him a send-off.

"How do I look?" he asked and she promptly answered, "Beautiful!"

"Aw, cut it out. I mean is my tie straight, collar neat— all that stuff?"

While Julie was reassuring him, Marilyn came by, interrupting her daily dash to the laundry to stop beside them.

"Da—vid!" she squeaked. "Do you look sharp! What's up?"

"He has an interview for a job," Julie said happily.

"What as? Mayor?" Marilyn leaned forward to inspect him from the side. Dave reached for her tempting pony tail, but already she was on her way.

"I'll vote for you," she called back. "Good luck!"

"That nut!" Dave grinned.

Julie, seeing the spark back in his eyes and the sullen line gone from his lips, was nearly undone, and summoned Signora Petrucelli's training to keep her voice even. "Smile like that and you can't lose."

"I won't lose. There's no competition." Dave meant that this job had not been listed in an employment agency. "All the same, keep your fingers crossed."

Julie thrust her crossed fingers into the air. "Till I hear from you. Call me as soon as you know."

"I will. 'Bye."

Much too ebullient just to go home, Julie returned to the school building to look for Anna.

"Do something with me," she begged when she found her. "Dave's gone for a job and I'll bust if I don't have someone to talk to."

"Golly, Julie, I have to study. Next week's exams and I'm scared."

"Come on up to my house and study," Julie suggested, and as an inducement added, "There's some chocolate cake."

"Twist my arm." Anna laughed. "I can see myself studying with you around, but all right."

On her front porch Julie really tried to let Anna study, but as the afternoon wore on with no word from Dave, she could not help interrupting.

"I wonder how he's making out." "How long does an interview take, anyway?" "Was that the phone?" "He should have called by now."

"Julie, shut—up! Here, if you must talk, ask me questions." Anna handed over her history book. "Start with the ones at the end of Chapter 1."

By quarter past five, Dave still had not called and Anna, collecting her books, said she simply must go. She paused at the edge of the porch. "Don't worry, Julie. He'll call."

"I know, but when?"

Anna burst into laughter. "There was a time when you worried about whether he'd even look at you, and now all you ask is will he call at five or six."

"But that job's so important to him," Julie said.

Anna leaned against the porch rail. "So that's the secret."

"What secret?" Julie asked.

"Of going steady. You care more about what he wants than what you want yourself, don't you?"

"I don't know." Julie thought of her singing. "I care about both, I guess. You don't want to go steady though, do you?"

"Me? Ha! Ha! Nobody ever takes me seriously. Anna Jensen, always good for laughs."

"You're crazy, Anna. Everyone likes you. Just pick out

one fellow and concentrate." Julie pulled herself up to sit on the rail. "Who would you choose?"

"You'll die when you hear." Anna lowered her voice. "Rickie Sheridan."

"Rickie Sheridan!" The arch enemy. "Why do you like him?"

"I dunno. Why does any girl like a certain fellow? Why do you like Dave, for instance?"

Why do I like Dave? After Anna had gone, Julie, in a glow of affection, asked herself that question. He was hot tempered and often bitter, sometimes against her, but he could be gentle too. His smoldering nature might burst into violence but it could also flame into contagious excitement, so that his look, his light touch, could raise her to a peak of delight. He was vital, that was it. Through all his groping, through every setback, he had never lost his core of strength. Power! He would get his power. Julie said a little prayer that he would not use it for his own destruction.

If he could land this job . . . She could wait no longer and hurried into the house and toward the phone. It rang before she reached it and when she answered, Dave's voice came, vibrant, over the wire. "Julie?"

"Dave! How did it go?"

"Good, I think. They didn't say definitely, but it looks as if I'm in."

Julie eased herself to the floor and settled back against the wall. "Tell me all about it."

"Well, first I filled out an application, then I talked to the personnel manager and he sent me to the head of the department where I'd work. I don't think he would've done that if he wasn't interested, do you?"

"I'm sure he wouldn't," Julie said.

"They just want to check my records at school. My marks aren't too bad and my athletic record is—well, mostly good."

"You'll make it, Dave. How could you miss?"

"They said . . . Say, Julie, how about a date tonight?"

"Tonight?" She hadn't done her practicing.

"I know it's a school night, but this is special." Dave chuckled. "Your first date with a businessman."

"I haven't done any work," Julie said. "Could you come over later, say about nine o'clock?"

"You and your conscience! How did I ever get mixed up with you?"

Above the mouthpiece Julie's eyes sparkled. "You tell me and we'll both know."

That night and the following day, Julie was borne along on the current of Dave's expectation. Around school he looked so genial that some of the fellows dared to say, "Hi," and what was more, Dave responded. But the morning after that he stormed into the school and with only a curt greeting to Julie, went directly to the office. She did not find him until after the third period.

"I'm getting out of here," he told her.

"Dave! What's happened?"

"Come over to The Hangout. I'll tell you."

Julie had never cut a class in her life, but she did not hesitate now. Running to keep up with his angry stride, hugging the books which he had not offered to carry, she followed him into the glare of the summer morning and down the sun-baked steps of the school. It was not till they reached the street that he began his enraged report.

"I didn't get the job."

"Why not? You were practically sure of it."

"Yeah. That was before they'd checked my school records. Temperamental. On-and-off. Poor citizenship rating."

"Dave! After all you've done for the school."

"A lot they care! There are laws against job discrimination, Julie, but they've fixed that. They get you before you even try for a job. Poor citizenship! How would they act if everyone was against them?"

"Everyone's not against you," Julie said helplessly. "Some people, maybe, but not everyone."

"You're a babe in arms," Dave scoffed. "Some day you'll find out and then you'll come over to my side."

"Stop running!" Julie fumbled for her handkerchief to wipe the perspiration from the back of her neck. "I am on your side."

"Yeah! Love 'em. Play up to 'em. Not me. I'm going right down and give that personnel manager a piece of my mind."

"Dave, no. That'll only make things worse."

"So what?"

The Hangout in late morning was quite a different place from the uproarious haunt known to the after-school crowd. As they pushed through the swinging door into an Arctic blast of air conditioning, Julie saw that there were only three customers at the counter, all men, and one clerk, a pasty-faced fellow she had not seen there before. With Dave at her side, she walked to the back of the room and slid into the last of the empty booths.

In the unusual quiet all sounds were magnified, the voice of a sports announcer on the low-tuned radio, the sizzle of hamburgers and the chatter of the clerk. Julie could see that the clerk talked over his shoulder as he worked, but Dave, with his back to the counter, could only hear the continual prattle. Annoyed, he leaned out of the booth and bellowed, "How about a little service?"

"Hold your horses," the clerk retorted. "Can't you see I got other customers?"

"White customers," Dave snorted to Julie. "We can wait."

Eventually the clerk came toward them, his rubber soles scrunching over the floor with maddening deliberation. At their table he bent to set down their water glasses but at that moment a blast of cheers came over the radio and he straightened, the glasses still in his hands.

"What happened?" he called to the men at the counter. "Home run?"

Dave's reaction was immediate. "What is this?" he

shouted. "A lunch joint or a baseball game? We'll have two hamburgers and two chocolate malts and make it snappy."

"Listen, big shot!" The clerk slammed the heavy glasses onto the table, and water splattered over its shiny surface. "If you're in such a sweat, why'n't you sit at the counter?"

Dave half rose, his arms stiff at his sides. "I said make it snappy."

Julie hurried to put in a placating word. "It's just that we have to get back to school."

The clerk's shifty eyes shot toward Julie and back to Dave. "Okay, okay," he said, and whether because of the breadth of Dave's shoulders or because of Julie's mediation, he retreated with haste.

"See?" Dave was triumphant. "You gotta get tough."

Beyond the clerk, Julie could see the men at the counter, three pairs of shoulders twisted toward her, three faces staring with condemnation. She reached out her hand to pull herself into the corner of the booth out of their sight, but slowly the hand slid back into her lap. Her face burned; in the clammy room, perspiration broke out on her body but she did not flinch. She was part of this, with Dave in his suffering, and right or wrong she would stand by him.

⪻ 17 ⪼

"Boy!" said Slim. "this is the way to live." he leaned back against a tree and pulled his pipe from his pocket.

"Then why do you have to go 'way?" Marilyn hitched herself along the ground, nearer to Slim. "We could have more picnics like this, take in some shows, go dancing . . ."

"Slim wants to see the world." Dave spoke from a reclining position. "Hey, Julie, what's the rush? We can clean up later."

"Ants." Julie picked up a piece of watermelon rind and dropped it into a paper bag.

Slim said New England was hardly the world, but he had this friend up there he wanted to visit and his vacation seemed like a good time to do it.

"But you don't have to stay two weeks. You could come back Wednesday or Thursday. Couldn't you?" Marilyn wheedled.

Was there actually a flick of annoyance before Slim's quick smile? He pulled Marilyn close and rubbed his cheek up and down against her hair with embarrassing intimacy. Julie, uncomfortable, crumpled up her refuse bag and turned to Dave. "Let's you and I go for a walk."

"Why can't you let a guy relax?" Dave sat up, stretching. "You want to go for a walk, Slim?"

"Are you kiddin'?" Slim released Marilyn to light his pipe. "I like it here."

"Remind me to find myself a nice easygoing girl." Dave rose to his feet. Julie threatened him with the bag, but he snatched it from her and tossed it to the ground. "Okay. Let's go."

They climbed down the bank to the dirt road above which they had picnicked. As soon as they were out of the others' hearing, Dave said, "Marilyn better watch it. A fellow doesn't like a girl to be so possessive."

Julie defended her friend. "She has a right to be possessive. They've been going together long enough."

"No longer than you and I. You try that with me and I'll hit you over the head."

"David Ross! I won't speak to you again this afternoon." Julie stamped off ahead of him.

Dave seemed to enjoy the situation. He made no effort to catch up but walked slowly behind her and teased her with a childhood chant. "Julie's mad and I am glad. Julie is a sorehead."

Pretending anger, Julie did not slacken her pace.

"Julie wishes I'd reform. Julie's always nagging." Dave's tone was still singsong but his words were barbed. Julie whirled toward him.

"Oh, for Pete's sake! Can't you ever let up? Can't you ever kid any more?"

"All right, all right. But how would you like it if someone came along and tore your house down?"

"I know," Julie said sympathetically. "But that has nothing to do with . . . I mean, it's happening to a lot of people."

That was true, of course. Homes and stores, playing fields and bowling alleys had been appropriated to make room for the new highway. It was a real hardship, especially for people like the Rosses who, over the years and bit by bit, had made themselves an attractive well-loved home. And it was unfortunate that the blow had fallen so soon after Dave's job rejection, that the highway people had called on his father that same week. Still, it was a big impersonal project and not, as Dave seemed determined to assume, an express affront to him and his family.

Julie had pointed this out many times in the past two weeks, but she tried again. "They didn't just pick you."

"Sure, sure. Then why did they skip the Sheridans? Highway's only going to miss their place by a few yards."

"Don't be such a mule! Do you actually believe they sat down and said, 'Look, the Rosses live here and the Sheridans there, so this is where we'll build our road'?" Julie took a skipping step to catch up with Dave. "Besides, it's not such a break for them. How would you like to live smack on the highway, with cars swishing by all the time?"

"Hey, yeah! I never thought of that." Dave spoke with

malevolent triumph and turned to Julie with a smile that was not a smile, with a glint in his eyes that made her shudder. "Wait till Rickie figures that one out!"

The idea cheered him and he walked with a new buoyancy, gloating happily. Julie listened in distressed silence until he said, "Aw, don't be sore. School's over, it's a beautiful day, and we have this whole road to ourselves."

"Yes." Julie thought of Dave's little sister who at church that morning had begged him to bring her along. "Maybe we should have let Penny come, though."

"What for?" Dave said. "Don't you think I want to be alone with my girl?"

"Now who's being possessive?"

"That's different," Dave said smugly. "I'm a fellow."

"Well, if that's not masculine conceit!" Julie stopped to face him, hands on hips, head thrown back in challenge. Dave pushed his fist against the tip of her nose and they both laughed.

It was a jewelled moment. She slipped her hand into his and smiled at the secret knowledge that she, too, was glad they were alone. Here on this woodland road, sun-spattered and still, they were just a boy and girl, young and together, and for this little while the problems of their everyday life could be pushed aside.

How few such moments there were in the hours and days and weeks of that summer! Contracts for the construction of the highway were let early in July, and the Rosses were requested to vacate within six weeks.

"What's their rush?" Dave stormed. "Are roads more important than human beings?"

"But how can they do it so fast?" Julie asked. "I don't see how they can possibly reach your house in that little time."

"Power, again. Money and machines and men. Men!" Dave, pacing the floor of Julie's living room, stopped abruptly. "They'll need lots of workers, Julie. Maybe there's my job."

They did need workers, strong ones with stamina and muscles like Dave's. Brawn and not attitude counted here and Dave was hired the day he applied. Julie admired his resourcefulness, the way he had made an opportunity out of misfortune, but he rejected her praise.

"Day laborer!" he snorted. "I'll kill myself in the boiling sun while Sheridan sits all comfortable and cool in a nice soft office job."

"Yes, but from what I've heard, you'll make a lot more money," Julie pointed out.

"Hey! Are you sure of that?"

Julie nodded helplessly, for again that ugly grin was spreading over his face.

~⚡~

Dave went to work and the palms of his hands blistered, then hardened. As it became evident that his family was being driven to homelessness, his mind and heart hardened too; his resolve for vengeance was whipped to greater strength as it grew to encompass the mother and father and sister who could find no place to live.

"Why can't they?" he demanded of Julie. "There's no shortage of houses, is there?"

"N-no." Julie had given up arguing with him.

"They have the money," Dave said. "That's one thing the highway people did, was pay enough for our house. My dad's perfectly honest. My gosh! He's been in the same job for thirty years. There's nothing wrong with my mother either. So why won't anyone sell us a house?"

Why? Julie knew the answer, but deep fear kept her from putting it into words. If this could happen to a quiet respectable family like the Rosses, it could happen to any Negro family, hers, for instance, and what good would a friendly approach do then? Her father had made a re-spected place for himself in the community, was greeted cordially on its streets and welcomed to its boards and com-mittees. But what if he should need a home? Would not his friends, like hers at the country club, merely stand by, sorry perhaps, but apathetic?

As if Dave's turmoil were not enough, Marilyn, too, was plagued by desperation. Slim returned from his vaca-tion and talked seriously of moving to New England.

"All that space," he told them. "Miles of woods and fields. Mountains. Whole villages of houses with wide lawns. Why be cooped up in a stuffy apartment?"

The possibility of losing Slim, and the long hot days at the laundry drove Marilyn to a frenzy of pleasure seeking, and she pulled them all into fevered activity. They rode on every roller coaster within an eighty-mile radius; they danced to every juke box and once, on a Sunday, climbed a mountain. Slim protested every step of the way, but Marilyn only laughed. "You wanted a mountain. So here's your mountain."

Oddly enough it was the fun-loving Slim who usually called a halt. "Let's take it easy for once," he would say. "Go up to Julie's and just sit."

So they would go to Julie's and Marilyn would "sit" for perhaps ten minutes before she rolled back the rugs and set the record player to blaring with dance music. Or she would push Julie to the piano and they would all sing, shouting at the tops of their lungs.

Julie never shouted, never for one moment forgot the need to protect her voice. In the midst of all this turbulence, music was her sanctuary and she tended it carefully and well.

It was not pure joy. Signora Petrucelli had gone abroad for the summer, and without the stimulus of lessons, the daily routine of exercises was often monotonous and dull. There were long periods of discouragement when Julie seemed to be making no progress. Then would come a day when every note and cadenza would sound exactly as she intended, and her elation would be boundless. Surely, surely, she would make Juilliard, and a year from now she could escape forever into the world of music.

On the fifteenth of August, Penny Ross was nine years

old. Julie, who often took care of the little girl while her folks were house hunting, decided to give her a party. Penny provided a guest list which turned out to include both white and colored children.

The party was a big success. The children ran all over the Brownells' lawn, played together, fought and made up, shared in eating impossible quantities of ice cream and cake. Late in the afternoon, Dr. Brownell came in to chauffeur them home, and for a few minutes stood beside Julie and watched the children.

"Look at them," Julie said. "All good friends. Why can't it stay this way?"

"I think it can some day," Dr. Brownell said. "It will take time, though, and a lot of patience."

Patience! How could you be patient when a nine-year-old child was practically without a home, when you must say to her, "Leave your presents here. You'll be moving soon and then I'll bring them to you."

Bring them where? To what place could she move? The Rosses had given up the idea of a house and tried the public housing projects, which they knew to be one of the few areas open to all races. Finding no vacancies, they turned to the dismal cold-water flats, but these were already dangerously overcrowded.

The highway was practically at their door when a house was found. At the time of its purchase, Mr. Ross was at work, Mrs. Ross in her kitchen. No one in the family had seen the house except as they drove past it. It was in a white neighborhood in which, as is often the case, there was a covenant among the property owners not to sell to anyone outside their own race. But no one suspected that the ruddy-faced lawyer who signed the contract was acting as intermediary for the sexton of his church. The lawyer was Mr. Halliday.

Dave's fury reached a new peak. "Patronage!" he ranted. "How could my father accept such a thing? Doesn't he have any pride?"

"What else could he do?" Julie asked. "He needed a home."

"He can have it. They can all have it. I won't go near the place," Dave vowed.

"But Dave! What will you do?"

"I don't know." Dave dropped his head and rubbed his hand across his eyes. When he spoke again, his voice broke. "I don't know."

Julie had never seen him defeated, and it made her ache with compassion. In that moment she would have given anything for the belligerent defiance against which she had argued, from which she had suffered. Perversely, she was not pleased when Dave, having moved into the house with his family, pulled out of his slump and was ready once more to fight his one-man battle.

It was a relief to get back to school, to the joy of re-union, to the rushing, often-interrupted exchanges of news, to all the familiar sights and sounds and smells. Senior year! This year Julie was among those who directed lost freshmen along the corridors, who had an established place in one of the biggest clubs, who moved easily from group to group in the yard. This year she belonged.

She did not see much of Dave that first week because he always had to hurry home to help his mother get settled in the new house. On Friday afternoon he invited her for Cokes, but she was on her way to her music lesson, her first since June.

"I can't wait to see whether Signora Petrucelli thinks I've improved," she said.

Dave was kidding her about her voice being a tough rival for him when, from behind them, someone called his name. Oh dear! It was Rickie Sheridan.

"Say, Dave," he said when he caught up with them. "The season hasn't started yet, but some of us thought we'd change and take a few turns around the track."

Dave glowered. "You can take your track team and go to the devil!"

Rickie looked surprised, then angry. "Listen to me, Ross. So you got a dirty deal last spring, but it wasn't our fault, was it? If you'd just take that chip off your shoulder . . ."

Dave did not wait for him to finish. He took one step toward Rickie, face set in hard lines, fists ready to fight. "Take that back!"

Julie did not think at all. She stepped between the two

boys and glared up at Rickie. "What right have you to speak to Dave like that? How would you feel if your best friend turned against you? How would you act if someone accused you of throwing games? Would you be all friendship if you got thrown out of a party and not one single person stood by you? You can just take your stupid smile somewhere else, Rickie Sheridan. You're nothing but a chicken-hearted hypocrite!"

Rickie was flabbergasted. So was Dave. Rickie stood there gaping, and behind Julie, Dave did not move.

It was Rickie who spoke first. "I—I'm sorry. I hadn't thought of all those things. Dave, I—apologize."

Only then did Julie realize what she had done. Only then was she aware of the crowd that had gathered, of all those faces, some fascinated, some frightened, some sneering. Sneering at her, at Julie Brownell, who had stood in a public place and screeched like a fishwife. Without another word she pushed through the crowd and walked out the gate.

Dave came after her. She heard his footsteps, felt his hand on her arm as he pulled her around to face him. "Julie!" He was beaming. "Julie, you fought!"

Julie's anger flared up again. "Yes, I fought and I hope you're satisfied. You got me into this, David Ross, and I never want to see you again."

She broke away and hurried up the street. At the first crossing she stopped, dazed. Where was she going? This was not the way to her house.

"Oh!" she said and again, "Oh!" How could she have been so thoughtless? Right on her way to her music lesson, to the moment toward which she had worked all summer, she had strained her voice. She had screamed.

✤ 18 ✤

"As you all know, we have some important business today." Miss Adams, the music teacher, smiled at the girls in her homeroom. "Nominations for this room's representative to the student council."

Immediately Beverly Blake jumped to her feet. "I nominate Julie Brownell."

Almost before Julie could believe she had heard correctly, Anna Jensen had seconded the nomination. An odd silence followed. Julie clasped her hands on her desk and stared at the blackboard. Why were no further names suggested? Ordinarily there was a slate of three or four.

Miss Adams said, "Who else?"

Bets Hampton jerked out of her seat. "I nominate Beverly Blake."

No one seconded. What was going on around here? Bev was a natural for the council, prominent and popular in the school as well as the class. And how must she feel to have no one back her? Julie rose to stand in the aisle.

"I—if it's all right for another candidate to do it, I second the motion."

There were no more nominations, and Miss Adams reminded them that a vote would be taken on Monday, and dismissed the class. Everyone smiled at Julie on the way out, but it was Anna who slipped an arm through hers. "You're practically elected, Julie. I don't know what Bets is trying to pull because we've already talked it over and decided on you."

"But why?" Julie was honestly puzzled. She had held no offices in the school and besides, such honors always went to a girl who had the backing of a sorority.

"Because . . ." Anna hesitated. "Because you're a good sport. Whatever happens to you, you take it with a smile, but if someone else gets a dirty deal, you're ready to fight."

So this was the result of that disgraceful scene with Rickie Sheridan, which she had been so sure would destroy all she had built up over the years. Rickie! Julie snatched her arm from Anna's. By virtue of his position as senior class president, he would automatically become president of the student council as well.

"Oh!" she said. "What will Rickie say?"

"It was his idea, Julie. I told you he was a terrific guy. You practically took his head off, and instead of getting mad, he—well, I don't know what he thinks, but he's the one who suggested you to Bev."

"Honestly?"

Dave would not like this, not at all. Sure he would consider it a betrayal, Julie was afraid to tell him about it, though she knew this would place another brick on the wall that was growing between them. Of course she had not meant it when she said she never wanted to see him again, and they had patched things up before the day was over. But neither of them could honestly concede that the other was right about her method of attack on Rickie and, rather than quarrel, they had dropped the subject. To two people who had always talked everything over, this was a kind of estrangement.

Dave's response to her election on Monday was exactly as she had anticipated. When she left school, he was waiting at the gate, waiting to congratulate her in tones of utter disgust.

She tried to win him to her viewpoint. "You don't know how much this means to me."

"Hm."

His grunt put her on the defensive. "Can I help it if Rickie's the president?"

"I said congratulations, didn't I?"

"Yes, but you didn't mean it." When he did not answer, Julie said, "Would you really want me to give up a chance to be on the student council?"

"That's entirely up to you." Dave spoke with a finality that shut her out.

Well, she could not let him spoil her deep satisfaction. Three years ago she had entered this school practically friendless; her hope, her struggle had been to find a place in its pattern. To be a leader went beyond her most cherished dream. It was as if she had passed a milestone, as if one job had been accomplished and she was now free to work toward the next. Juilliard.

She could not let anxiety about Dave spoil that either, for on the coming Sunday she was to sing her first solo at church. Her lesson on that awful Friday had not been fatal after all. Though upset, she had not actually been hoarse, and on that very day Signora Petrucelli had suggested that she start regular solo work.

"So you'll be used to it by the time of the Juilliard audition, Julie. How about your choir? Will they give you an opportunity?"

"Yes, I'm sure they will." They had been after her for solos for the last year.

Her selection was to be *The Lord's Prayer* by Malotte, and all week she worked on it in a strange combination of growing confidence and trepidation. By Saturday night she had reached bursting point and looked forward to the relaxation of her usual date with Dave. But Dave did not call.

"Why don't you call him?" her mother suggested. "He never misses a Saturday night. Perhaps he's ill."

Julie was tempted, but pride kept her from the phone. She knew very well that he was in the best of health.

Troubled about Dave, nervous about her solo, she spent a restless night. By morning the thought of the solo crowded out everything else and formed such a knot in her stomach that she could eat no breakfast. On her way to church she sat in the back of the car, stiff and speechless.

Dr. Brownell left her and her mother at the door of the church regretfully. "I almost wish I weren't a doctor," he said. "I'd give a great deal to be there this morning."

"Maybe it's a good thing you can't." A slight chuckle loosened Julie's tension, but when the organ struck the first notes of her solo, it returned in full force. She rose to face the congregation, holding her music in clammy hands.

"*Our Father . . .*" No quiver!

"*Which art in Heaven . . .*" Gradually her nervousness drained away. As she grew used to the sound of her voice in the arched room, an awareness of her listeners crept over her. She did not see faces but felt a rapt attention, a rapport in harmony with her song.

When she was finished, church or no church, she had to smile down at her mother. After a year of lessons she was her own harshest critic and she knew she had done a good job.

She could hardly wait to get home and report to Daddy but she was waylaid by the many admirers who gathered around her. Penny Ross stayed beside her, clinging to her hand with proprietary pride, and Julie found a sort of secondhand pleasure in this support by a member of Dave's family. Dave had not been in church.

Nor was he at Youth Fellowship that evening. The next

Saturday they went to the movies with Marilyn and Slim but Dave was so distant he seemed a stranger.

Julie tried to tell herself that it did not matter, that with or without Dave she had plenty of friends and interests to fill her time. And there was the still incredible delight of being on the student council.

At the end of its second meeting, Rickie asked her if she could stay a few minutes longer. When the others had left he said, "Julie, I especially wanted you on this council because I thought we needed your point of view."

"About what?" Julie knew of no plans for school musical events.

"About—remember the day you told me off? I said I hadn't thought of all those things, but that wasn't altogether true. I had thought some, especially since that country-club deal."

"I see." Julie turned away. It still disturbed her to be pointed up as a Negro.

"That party was perfectly obvious, but there must be other things, things we can't know unless you tell us."

Julie picked a splinter from the desk at her side. "There's nothing."

"There must be," Rickie insisted. "For instance, I didn't see why Dave got sore when I started going with Bets Hampton, never got wise that he thought I meant to ditch him. Heck! You know how it is. We can all be friends, but in this town, we just don't double date."

Aroused at last, Julie whipped around to face him.

"Anna Jensen would." She could have bitten off her tongue! Anna would not welcome this plug in her behalf.

Rickie said, "Jensen? Oh, that girl in my English class. I don't know her very well, but listen. I think if we bring these problems into the open, maybe we can do something about them. I'd like to straighten it out with Dave, too. Can you get him to talk to me?"

"I'll see."

Julie felt terribly let down. Her triumph had not been a personal victory after all; they had chosen her, not for herself, but because she was a Negro. She could only hope she was breaking the ice for others, that a day might come when they would be used to an interracial council and select their members for their merits alone.

As for Rickie, he could go fly a kite. She was not going to air her problems publicly, or Dave's or anyone else's. She would not relay the message, either. Maybe she should, but why risk Dave's anger? Their relationship was precarious enough as it was.

By the time Rickie spoke to her about it again, her contacts with Dave had become limited to an occasional brief encounter at school, and she merely said, "I haven't asked him."

Rickie scratched a spot behind his ear. "Is it because— you didn't mind my talking that way, did you?"

Julie shook her head, as much in impatience as negation. Why should she be spokesman for her race?

Rickie stared at her thoughtfully and she tried to think

of a way to change the subject, but he was the one to introduce a new note. "By the way, I've been getting acquainted with that Jensen girl. Nice kid."

"Oh yes, she is!" Julie was glad, after all, that she had sparked Rickie's interest in Anna. It was more fun to play Cupid than mediator. It would be nice if she could fix everyone's affairs, could quell Marilyn's apprehension every time Slim spent a week end in New England and, for herself, recover her old relationship with Dave.

At Marilyn's suggestion, she tried going out with other boys. With Joe Peters, the shy little fellow with whom she had danced in the Paul Jones at her first church party. Joe was dull and a doormat and only made her long for the vigor of Dave. With Stan Raymond, new to the church group, whose good looks and self-assurance had caused such a splash among the girls. Stan made rough advances which frightened her and only made her long for the security of Dave.

But she still had her music, and her progress was a constant source of encouragement. On the Sunday after Thanksgiving she reached a new first. The choir director had given her a number of solos but never before the solo part of an anthem.

She went to church alone that day because her mother was laid up with a virus infection. As she waited for the bus, she twisted and untwisted the handle of her purse, and walked back and forth with quick little steps. Would she never get over these pre-performance jitters? Signora

Petrucelli said it was a good sign, that one could not do her best unless she was keyed up to it. Still she hated to think of spending the rest of her life with this gone-in-the-middle feeling.

Oh, stop worrying, she scolded herself. It went well in rehearsal, didn't it?

It went well in performance, too, and Julie found it an exhilarating experience. The responsibility of her part combined with the support of the other singers stimulated her to new mastery and she returned to her seat in a glow.

After the service, as usual, she was surrounded by people who wished to express appreciation and, also as usual, Penny stood at her side to share the honors. One little old lady told her she was an inspiration, and Penny snickered.

"I guess children just don't get inspired." Julie put her arm across Penny's shoulders so that the little girl would not feel squelched by her words. Still in this position they left the building and Julie, looking down at Penny, did not notice the car parked a few yards from the church.

"There's Dave!" Penny shrieked. "He came to get us. Come on, Julie. He'll take you too."

"Oh no, not today, thanks," Julie said, but by then Mrs. Ross had rolled down the back window and was calling out to her.

"Come along, Julie. We'll give you a lift."

There was no escape. Penny, protesting loudly that she wanted to sit by Julie, was hauled into the back seat by her mother, and Julie slid in beside Dave.

"Hi," she said.

" 'Lo." Dave stepped on the gas and eased the car away from the curb.

Mrs. Ross said, "You were lovely this morning, Julie. David, you should have heard her."

"Dave's a bad boy," Penny announced. "Won't never go to church."

"Won't ever," Dave corrected curtly, and to Julie he muttered, "At least you're singing in your own church."

"Where else would she sing?" Penny demanded.

To cover the awkward moment, Julie twisted around toward Penny. "You wait. Some day you'll hear me in the Metropolitan Opera House."

"Where's that?" Penny wanted to know.

As she answered Penny's questions and chatted with Mrs. Ross, Julie wondered what Dave was thinking. She wished she could ask him about himself. Had he found a substitute for athletics? For her? He was smart enough to get decent marks without much study. What did he do with the rest of his time?

They were nearly home when Mrs. Ross said, "I wish you'd get David out more, Julie. All that boy does is sit in the house and read."

Julie saw Dave's lips tighten but had to say something. "What have you been reading, Dave?"

"Books."

His abrupt answer sent Penny into a fit of giggles so contagious that Julie had to smile. "You might enjoy

Youth Fellowship tonight," she said. "We're having a speaker from the N.A.A.C.P."

"What's N.A—N.A—what's that?" asked the irrepressible Penny.

"National Association for the Advancement of Colored People," Dave snapped. He slowed to a stop at the foot of Julie's steps.

Julie turned to say good-bye to Mrs. Ross and Penny, and her right hand reached for the handle of the door.

"David!" Mrs. Ross spoke sharply. "Help Julie out. Where are your manners, boy?"

"That's all right," Julie said, but Dave had already yanked open his door and started around to her side of the car. He waited while she stepped out and followed her across the walk and up the first few steps of the stairway.

"Look," he said. "I know about that speaker tonight and I'll be there. But you'd better stay away."

"Why?"

"Because it's the National Association for the Advancement of Colored People. You won't even admit you are colored."

"Da—" she started, but he had left. She could only stand there rigid with unspoken anger. What right did he have to say a thing like that? How could she help admitting her color when every time she looked in a mirror she saw a brown face? When Rickie and Dave, himself, made such a point of talking about it? Dave was crazy. Just plain crazy!

The sound of the motor cut off her mental tirade. She saw the car jerk to a start and swerve sharply into a turn. Dave was angry too. At her. He had scolded—at her. Would he care what she thought if he did not like her at all?

The car backed, turned again, and started down the street. Penny waved from the window and Julie waved back. Waved and sighed. What good did it do to have him care, when she could find no way to reach him?

✗ 19 ✗

AFTER DAVE'S CHALLENGE THERE WAS LITTLE THAT COULD have kept Julie from Youth Fellowship that night. But that little happened late in the afternoon when Marilyn arrived at the house, her eyes red-rimmed and puffy. Slim had gone, had found the long-sought job in New England, and come home only long enough to pack his clothes.

Marilyn was desolate. "What'll I do? What'll I do without Slim?"

"You'll find someone else," Julie comforted. "A girl like you. All you have to do is smile and the boys come running."

"I don't want boys! After Slim, the kids I know at school seem like a bunch of babies."

Julie searched her mind for some other consolation. "What about art?"

"Who cares about that?" Marilyn said.

Her apathy stabbed at Julie. She had meant to help keep Marilyn's ambition alive but somehow she had failed. She had failed Dave too. Why? What had she done that was wrong? If your skin was brown you had to make sure that it was also tough; you had to work twice as hard for what you wanted. Why couldn't Dave see that? Or Marilyn?

By the next morning Marilyn's agitation had subsided but she did not bounce back as she had in the past. Listless and indifferent, she went from school to the laundry and took no interest in breaking her monotonous routine. Julie tried to draw her into the choir, which needed extra members for the Christmas Sunday Candelight Service, but Marilyn only shrugged and said, "What for?"

She did not even attend the service, but Dave did. From the choir loft Julie spotted him sitting with his mother and Penny, and for once it was all she could do to concentrate on singing. What had brought him here today? Had the good will of the season softened his grudge against the world? Against her?

In the recessional she walked with slow dignity, but the lighted taper in her hand shook a bit when she passed Dave's pew. She allowed herself one quick look in his direction. He was watching her, his face impassive.

The second the final *Amen* was over, she blew out her candle and headed for the stairs, pulling off her choir robe as she ran. Though delayed by compliments on her solo work and exchanges of Christmas greetings, she was back in the entryway before a quarter of the congregation had left. The young people had begun to gather on the far side of the door. Dave was among them! Maybe today he would seek her out.

"Hey, Julie," someone called. "We're all going somewhere. You got any ideas?"

Dave, too? "You can come to my house," she suggested. "We can stop and get stuff to eat on the way."

"What do you know?" One of the fellows snapped his fingers. "Just like that, we've got a party."

"You have a job," Julie retorted. "Wait'll you make about a hundred sandwiches."

As they stood around making plans, Dave edged his way to Julie and spoke to her stiffly. "Your singing was very good."

"Thank you." Julie buttoned, then undid the top button of her coat. "I—hope you'll come to the party."

"Maybe."

They were separated by the Youth Fellowship president, who was organizing transportation. Julie took a bunch of girls in her father's car and did not know whether Dave would come until he turned up at the house. The boys had taken on the shopping and came in loaded with bread and cold cuts and cheese and enough Coke to flood the Sahara. This was going to be a party!

The Brownells' house could have accommodated everyone comfortably had they not all insisted on packing into the kitchen. Sarah Lou caught their spirit and wanted to whip up a batch of cookies but did not stand a chance. Julie, tossing a salad, answering repeated shouts for the salt or a knife or spoon, never lost track of Dave. He stood against the wall and chatted with this one or that but made no effort to participate.

"Julie! We've run out of butter. You got any?"

"Uh—what? Butter? Look in the refrigerator." She had better concentrate on being a hostess.

Despite Dave's indifference, it turned out to be one of the best parties Julie had ever had. They ate and played games and danced and sang. Occasionally someone left, a girl with an early curfew or a couple who wanted to be alone, but there were still quite a few around when they decided they were hungry again and raided the refrigerator.

It was long after midnight when they broke up. Dave intended to leave with the others and was pulling on his coat when one of the fellows said with a wink, "What's the matter with you? Aren't you going to help Julie with the dishes?"

Dave glanced at Julie, but the others would allow him no uncertainty. They yanked off his coat and only tossed it back as they went out the door.

Left alone, both he and Julie were ill at ease. Julie said, "Let's sit. I'm beat."

Dave muttered something about the dishes but Julie had already started toward the davenport. She flopped onto it and kicked off her shoes. "I missed Marilyn tonight. Didn't you?"

"Yeah." Dave sat beside Julie, though not near her.

"That Slim!" Julie said. "He's made her so unhappy!"

"You can't blame him," Dave argued. "All the same, I don't think he has the answer. What good does it do to move to another town?"

"The answer?"

"I don't know what the answer is, though," Dave said. "I've read a lot of books, even went to an N.A.A.C.P. meeting. Guess who's the first person I saw?"

"Who?"

"Mr. Halliday."

"What in the world was he doing there?" Julie asked.

"Yeah, what? They can't even leave us alone in our own organization."

Julie sat up straight. "They must want to help, then. Mr. Halliday, for instance. He's been a good friend to your family, Dave."

"Sure. So he can go home and pat himself on the back."

"Oh, forget Mr. Halliday. What can we do for Marilyn?"

Dave ignored her. "He told my father I ought to study law. Join the great fight for racial equality. I'll fight, all right, but not the way he wants." Dave had been addressing the opposite wall but now he looked at Julie. He stood up and patted her shoulder. "I'm sorry. I know you don't like this kind of talk."

"I don't mind." Julie reached for her shoes and set them side by side, next to the davenport. Dave said he'd better take off and she saw him to the door, walking beside him in her stocking feet.

"Seriously," she said, "don't you know some fellow Marilyn might like?"

"Oh, listen! She'll have to find her own boy friend."

"She likes older fellows," Julie mused. "George!"

"Who's George?"

"You know. My cousin," Julie reminded him. "Marilyn's always liked him, and he likes her, too. I could ask them both up here. Would you—no, I guess you wouldn't want to."

"Want to what?"

"I was going to ask if you'd come too. It would be less obvious if we had a foursome."

"Sure I'll come," Dave said. "I'd like to meet that George."

The matchmaking effort was a success. Marilyn brightened at the sight of George and thereafter her conversation was punctuated with "George says," and "George thinks." What Julie had not foreseen was the effect on Dave. George offered the outlet on the verge of which he had so often teetered. George was older and thus to be admired. George was the ally for whom he had sought.

Julie saw little of Dave for a while but noticed his occasional absences from school and heard from Marilyn when he and George had made a killing with dice or at pool. If only she had encouraged him the night he had spoken of studying law! He had been groping for a solution to his problems, and she had unwittingly given him the worst possible answer.

Toward the end of January George and Dave invited Julie and Marilyn to go dancing. Julie went but did not enjoy it. Like a chameleon, Marilyn always adapted herself to the young man of the moment and while with Slim she had been lighthearted and gay, with George she was noisy and a little coarse. Dave, too, followed George's lead, and all evening they made an exhibition of themselves.

At least Julie had not put a damper on their fun, because a couple of weeks later they asked her to go again. At first she made an excuse, something about singing the next day, but Dave looked at her so accusingly that she gave in.

When he came up to get her, the snow that had been falling in large flakes had turned to fine misty drops, almost like rain. Squinting against the wind, they felt their way through the drifts on the stairway and once fell, one on top of the other, and sat there laughing while snow melted icily over the tops of their boots and up their sleeves. It felt good to get into George's heated car.

George was an even more impatient driver than in his younger days, nor was he restrained by the blinding snow. Both Julie and Marilyn gasped every time he passed a car and headed into the misted glow of oncoming headlights. They narrowly missed more than one collision and each time George gloated, "Made it!" The others giggled and laughed, more from nerves than merriment.

The downtown section was a beautiful bedlam. Snow blew in sparkles past the lighted store windows and formed a diffused halo around every street and traffic light and an aura around each neon sign. But in the road, busses and cars were badly snarled, and drivers rolled down their windows to shout, or uselessly honked their horns.

George chafed at the delay and cursed indiscriminately at vehicles and red lights. Marilyn spurred him on. "Atta boy," she would say, or "That's telling 'em."

Julie tried to calm him. "There's no rush, George. We have the whole evening."

"Relax, Julie," Dave said. "With George it's always a rush." His tone was one of admiration.

They got through the jam at last and headed with comparative ease toward the roadhouse which was their destination. On the far side of town they hit one more red light and when it turned green, the car in front of them stalled. There was no way to pass it because of the stream of traffic from the opposite direction. George let out a string of oaths and leaned on his horn.

"He's stuck," Dave shouted over the noise. "Why don't you give him a push?"

Neither Dave nor anyone else expected George's response. Instead of easing against the stalled car, he stepped hard on the gas and smashed into it. At the moment, the other driver was stepping out, apparently to examine his motor, and the jar knocked him into the path of an oncoming car.

Everything happened so fast that Julie was hardly aware of what had taken place. She must have heard the screech

of brakes, seen the flash of swerving headlights and felt the
damp blast of air through the open door. Not until George
yelled, "The fool!" did she realize that Dave was rushing
toward the man who lay in the road and that she herself
was on the edge of her seat, biting hard on her mittened
fist.

"Shut the door!" George bellowed. "I'm getting out of
here."

It was Marilyn who cried, "You can't!" and indeed
there was no way. The nearest oncoming car had skidded
into a snow bank on the left curb, and the car behind that
had rammed into it and had slid around in the opposite
direction, so that the two formed a barricade.

"There's the sidewalk," George pointed out. "Shut that
door!"

The other driver, helped to his feet by Dave, was shaking his head in a dazed manner. Julie made no move to
shut the door. George tried to back out but his bumper
was locked.

It was amazing how quickly a crowd gathered on the
hitherto empty street. A policeman was among them, in-
vestigating, questioning, taking license numbers. The vic-
tim, a middle-aged Negro, claimed he was not hurt, insisted
over and over that it had been an accident and refused to
press charges. No witness knew what had actually occurred, and George was released. The policeman and some
of the bystanders helped untangle the cars and they drove
off.

George blustered, but only Marilyn encouraged him. Dave sat leaning forward on his seat and stared straight ahead. After a long time he spoke. "It was a colored man."

"Look!" George said. "Did I know the guy was gonna get out of his car?"

" 'Course not," Marilyn cooed.

Dave went on as if to himself. "It could have been my father."

"Oh, drop it!" George said angrily.

Julie, still shaky, longed for the touch of Dave's hand but sensed the struggle going on within him and did not intrude.

In the parking lot of the roadhouse, George looked over his shoulder. "Listen. Are we gonna go in there and have some fun or are we gonna mope all evening?"

Julie wanted to go home but waited for Dave to reply.

"It's up to you, George," he said.

"Okay." George turned off the motor. "Snap out of it and let's go."

Dave did not snap out of it and George, irked by the atmosphere of disapproval, soon gave up and they started home. Dave did not say a word all the way. It was not until he and Julie reached her porch that he started to talk.

"I guess you can't fight alone. You only hurt the wrong people."

Julie had no way of picking up the threads of his thoughts but she encouraged him softly. "I know."

"Personal revenge—maybe it helps your feelings but

not your race. You strike out blindly and—why, we might have killed that man! One of our own."

"But Dave, George wouldn't purposely . . ."

"I guess the only way is to join the group working for a fair deal through the courts." Dave's eyes were on Julie's face, but he did not seem to be looking at her. "Yes. My mind's made up. I'm going to study law."

The storm had stopped, but as he spoke a small avalanche fell from the roof and sprayed them with snow as it passed the porch. Julie felt as if a weight had fallen from her, too, and she reached up and laid a hand against Dave's cheek. "I'm glad. You'll make a wonderful lawyer."

Dave snatched the hand and crushed it between both his own. "Don't think I'm going to change."

"I don't want you to." Julie knew he must stay as he was. The fearlessness he had shown tonight, his aggressiveness, even his bitterness would be needed for the cause he had espoused. "I—I like you the way you are."

"You've done enough complaining," Dave reminded her.

"I won't any more," Julie promised. "Only—if you don't mind, you're practically breaking my wrist."

❧ 20 ❧

"THAT'S FINE, JULIE." MISS ADAMS TWISTED AROUND ON the piano bench and looked at Julie with admiration. "You've come a long way."

"Really do you think so?" Julie allowed herself one second, perhaps two, to ignore her own dissatisfaction with the way she had sung the aria. "I know it needs a lot more work but there's a whole month before the concert. So may I—try it?"

"Of course you may. And I'm sure you'll do all right." Miss Adams rose and gave Julie her music. "Remember, no one will expect perfection."

But I do, Julie thought. I'll make it perfect too. She thanked Miss Adams and scurried toward the door in a tingle. She was going to sing an operatic aria in the glee club's spring concert!

The rest of the club members had left before her audition and she was startled by a voice in the dim corridor outside the music room. "Success?"

"Oh! You scared me." Julie laughed, for it was only Anna. "Yes, she's going to let me do it."

"Told you so," Anna said. "You were a dope to think she mightn't."

"Maybe." But the uncertainty had made the triumph that much more rapturous, and when they left the building and saw the team down on the track oval, Julie wanted to tell Dave all about it.

"Let's watch the boys for a while," she suggested. "Maybe they'll walk us home."

"Too cold." Anna dug into her coat pocket and pulled out her gloves. "Who'd ever think this was the first day of spring?"

"You mean you wouldn't freeze for Rickie?"

"You've got me," Anna said, laughing. "Let's go."

The two girls skirted the oval and sat down on the bleachers. Julie leaned forward, resting her chin on one hand, and concentrated on Dave.

It was so good to see him out there with the others again. Once he had made up his mind to study law, he had gone about preparing for his career with complete singleness of purpose. To go to college he would need a scholarship; extracurricular activities might help him to qualify, and so he had gone back into athletics. Harder for him was the necessity for a good citizenship rating, but he had really tried to drop the chip from his shoulder and to a large extent had succeeded.

Rickie had helped, of course, had been willing to meet Dave on his own ground and renew their old friendship. If only the two boys would not argue all the time! They had the whole school discussing race relations, and it made Julie feel like Exhibit A.

She shivered and turned to Anna. "You were right about the weather. I'm congealed."

"Me too." Anna tucked her hands under her cuffs. "If this is your idea of devotion, you ought to be an Eskimo."

By the time track practice broke up, the girls' teeth were chattering and Rickie suggested that they wait inside. As they cut across the oval toward the gym, Julie maneuvered to get Dave apart from the others.

"Guess what," she said. "My solo has been decided on. 'My Heart at Thy Sweet Voice' from *Samson and Delilah*."

"Sounds impressive," Dave said, but he was plainly not impressed.

"I need the practice," Julie said defensively. "That's one of the songs I may be asked to sing in the Juilliard test."

"Who's complaining?"

"No one." But she had wanted him to share her pleasure. She'd been crazy to think he might, though, for he constantly belittled the value of her music. Those doors she hoped to open, he thought should be knocked down because, he said, a door which has been stuck for years will not yield to a gentle push. He had become such a crusader!

Seeing her disappointment, he tried to make amends. "Look, it's great about your solo. Cheer up." He pressed the flat of his hand against her forehead and the warmth of his palm made the class ring on his finger feel like a spot of ice against her skin. Rickie's ring was on a chain around Anna's neck.

Rickie called back to them to step on it and when they caught up with him, he said, "I don't suppose these girls risked pneumonia for no reason. Looks like we're stuck for a couple of hot chocolates. How about it, Dave?"

"Sure," Dave agreed.

As naturally as that they started to double date, for hot chocolates at The Hangout a couple of times led them to plan to see a movie together.

Julie knew Dave was reluctant to go, and it made her uneasy that the others did not show up on time. When they did arrive, all the seats were taken and they stood at the back of the theater for quite a while before the usher came to tell them he had two pairs in different rows if they cared to separate.

"Let's," Anna said. "My feet are killing me."

Julie and Dave walked down the aisle ahead of Anna and Rickie, and so it was Julie who started into the first row of seats to which the usher pointed with his flashlight. The gentleman on the end stood up to let her pass, but the woman next to him slouched down and pressed her knees against the seat in front.

"Excuse me, please," Julie whispered, but the woman did not budge.

The gentleman prodded her. "Mary, these people want to get by."

"Let 'em go somewhere else," the woman said aloud.

Julie started to back out but Dave pressed his hand hard between her shoulder blades. "Go ahead, Julie."

"Listen, lady . . ." That was Rickie's voice, tight and angry, but before he could finish, the usher intervened.

"Madam, I'll have to ask you to let them through."

The woman snorted and dropped her knees, plopping her feet against the floor with legs outstretched so that Julie and Dave had to climb over them.

Julie sank into her seat, burning with mortification. Why must Dave use her for a guinea pig? If he wanted to push in where he was not welcome, let him do it when she wasn't there. Sometimes he did not seem to consider her as a person at all.

Her mind had accused him too quickly, for as soon as he was settled he reached for her hand and gave it a sympathetic squeeze. At his touch, tears sprang to her eyes, blurring the colors on the screen. He had only done what he thought was right. But what about her standards? Were they so wrong? She and Dave had gained seats, but had they not made themselves unpleasantly conspicuous?

The incident touched off one of the incessant arguments between Rickie and Dave and afterward, having sodas, they went at it hot and heavy.

"It only proves what I've said all along," Rickie insisted. "You have to educate people."

"That takes too long!" Dave's fist crashed against the table. "I tell you we have to fight for our rights."

"So you fight. I know how many gains have been made through legal procedures, but tonight you had the law on your side and where did it get you?"

"It got me into a seat," Dave pointed out.

The verbal tussle went on and on. Julie picked up her spoon and traced designs in the froth on the inside of her glass, and Anna scrunched up the paper covers of their straws and dripped water onto them to make snakes. The froth hardened and the paper covers grew dank. Anna looked at Julie, raising her eyebrows in impatience, and tapped Rickie's knuckles.

"We're here," she reminded him.

Rickie glanced at her sidelong and returned his attention to Dave. "Of course you were right. I would've punched that woman in the . . . " Belatedly, Anna's signal registered and he stopped abruptly. " 'Scuse us, girls. I guess we do too much yakking."

Anna said she didn't mind but she never had seen what the fuss was all about. "My mother's German and my father's Danish and one of my aunts married an Italian. To me, people are people."

"Say that again!" Julie spoke emphatically. The trouble with Dave was he wanted to point up differences while she believed in seeking common ground.

She mentioned this to Dave when he took her home,

speaking cautiously, for he had almost made her doubt her own convictions. "Do you really think it's completely useless to—oh, you know—to try and knit people together? With something like music, for instance?"

"Is that honestly why you want to sing?" Dave demanded.

"Well—maybe only partly," Julie admitted. "I want to sing because I have to. But why can't it help make friends for us all?"

"Could be." Dave was noncommittal. "Oh, speaking of music, Penny asked me to remind you that you promised to help her with her piano piece for the school recital."

"I haven't forgotten," Julie said. "Why don't I bring her home from church with me tomorrow? She can have dinner with us."

"She'll be tickled silly. That kid adores you, Julie. Copies everything you do and say."

"I'll have to watch myself." Julie chuckled, but Dave was not fooling.

"Yes. It's quite a responsibility."

There was no mistaking the challenge in his tone. But what did he want of her? He knew she was no fighter, that the memory of her one outburst could still make her burn with shame.

During the Easter vacation her faith in herself was bolstered when she helped her father in his office. He had only colored patients and Julie was deeply impressed by the way his gentle sympathy sent them out with new hope and courage. She only wished Dave could have shared her experience, could have seen for himself that one could serve without belligerence.

Back at school, she found Anna rejoicing over a scholarship she had won for a secretarial course in New York, and Bev Blake excited because her senior prom committee had secured the services of Bill Manny's Band.

"We're lucky," Bev said. "Those colored . . ." Noticing Julie in the group, she broke off, flustered. "I mean, that band has so much rhythm."

Telling Dave about it later, Julie complained of Bev's always treating her as if she were breakable.

"But you ask for it," Dave said.

"Just what do you mean?"

"Figure it out for yourself." Dave changed the subject. "Where's Marilyn today?"

"How should I know?" Julie flared, but actually she was concerned about Marilyn's absence, and right after school went to the Halls' to check. Finding no one at home, she stopped at the nearest coin booth and phoned the laundry. Yes, Miss Hall was there, they said, but was not permitted to receive personal calls.

It was not like Marilyn to play hooky. Julie was anxious, and late in the afternoon decided to go to the laundry and wait for her. She would not be at work if she were ill, but perhaps she was upset about something and needed a friend.

Apparently Marilyn was not upset, for when she saw Julie, her only expression was one of surprise. "What are you doing here?"

"I was worried about you," Julie said. "Why weren't you at school?"

"You!" Marilyn laughed out loud. "I might have known you'd worry." She started down the street at Julie's side. "I'm quitting school."

"What!"

"Too much effort," Marilyn explained. "School, the laundry, housework, homework . . . Last week when we had vacation, I had time to breathe."

"But there are only two months to go," Julie protested.

"So what?" Marilyn said cheerfully. "What do I need of a high-school diploma?"

A memory shimmered across Julie's mind, the memory of a younger Marilyn strutting across the Brownells' living room, her voice softer then, and eager. *Wouldn't it be exciting if I turned out to be an artist?*

"Marilyn," she urged. "Don't give up art."

"Art!" Marilyn scoffed. "Where could I get without training?"

"Get training," Julie persisted. "Once you graduate you can find a better job and go to night school."

"Yah!" Marilyn said. "Like Lorraine."

Julie was taken aback. She had not thought of Lorraine in ages. Where was she now? Did she ever think of the younger sister she had entrusted to Julie's care?

Marilyn's moment of bitterness had passed. "It doesn't matter. Some day I'll be married and that, really, is what I want."

Julie could not pass it off so lightly. How awful to have to relinquish your dreams! She wondered whether the outcome might have been different if Lorraine had not given up the struggle to succeed as a Negro. Wouldn't her example have spurred Marilyn to further effort?

An example, that was it. *Penny copies everything you do.* Others might copy her, too, for every successful Negro set a pattern of hope for those who followed. This, then, was her answer to Dave.

"I know I'm no pioneer," she told him. "Lots of people have already paved the way. Only every one of us who wins respect gives reassurance to all the others."

"Yes, but you . . ." Again they were sitting on the bank of the river and Dave picked up a stone and tossed it into the water. "Look, I have nothing against your career, but I can't help thinking that, in your heart, you don't give a hoot for the others. Me, maybe, and Marilyn. Penny. But what you really want is acceptance for yourself."

"Naturally, I want people to like me," Julie said. "Don't you?"

"Not at the price of pretending I'm something I'm not!" Dave's hands gripped both her arms, and his voice, though low, was urgent and compelling. "You're a Negro, Julie. Face it. You can never help your race if you deny it."

Once before he had made this accusation but in a temper

which had brought only discord. This time his tone touched off a sympathetic vibration deep within her and she cried out to smother the sound.

"No, Dave! No! How could I deny what I am?"

ᶺᵉ 21 ᶺᵉ

DRIVING DOWN NEW YORK'S WEST SIDE HIGHWAY WITH
Dave, Julie was scarcely aware of her surroundings, of the
swish of traffic, of the wide river sparkling in the sun, of
the thick green foliage on the opposite shore. It was there-
fore remarkable that she broke her silence to ask, "Why
are all the American flags hung out?"

Dave laughed at her. "Wake up, Julie. For you it's the
day of the Juilliard test, but for everyone else it's Memorial
Day."

"Oh." Julie smiled faintly and slipped back into her
trance.

Dave tried to carry on a conversation, but she was so
unresponsive he finally gave up. "Oh, well," he said jok-
ingly. "I'll see you later."

There had been a time when a lull between them would
have bothered Julie, but this morning she did not notice
it. Nor did she once think of the challenge his presence
so often evoked. Face it. Face it. How many times had the
words popped, unbidden, into her mind! How often she
had pushed them back, promising herself to consider them

later! After the Juilliard test, after the prom, maybe not until after commencement.

The car in front of them stopped short and with almost one movement, Dave slammed on his brakes and thrust out his arm to keep Julie from being thrown forward.

"You all right?" he asked.

"I'm fine."

As he drew his hand back to the steering wheel, the flash of the sun on his class ring caught her eye, and the question of why he still withheld this symbol of his affection skimmed across the top of her mind. Even this did not trouble her, for today there was only one reality. The test.

She had been scared from her first moment of awakening, but when they drew up in front of the school, she was seized with such panic she could not move.

Dave said, "Well, here we are."

"Yes."

"Listen to me, Julie. Try to concentrate for just one minute. You don't know exactly when you'll be through and I don't know where I can find a spot for the car. So I'll meet you around four-thirty right over there." He pointed to the small park behind a high wall opposite the school.

"Hm?" Julie murmured. "Oh, yes. The park."

"Come to!" Dave chuckled, then grew serious and put his warm hand over her cold one. "Good luck, Julie. Very good luck."

His touch released her and she thanked him and got out

of the car. She stood on the sidewalk looking up at the long gray-white building and the sounds of music floated out to her, a voice, a clarinet and, far off, the tuning of a cello. This was Juilliard, the object of her hopes and dreams and hours of hard work. No matter how the test came out she was, for this one day, a part of it. Exhilarated, she hurried up the steps and crossed the threshold.

Though she was early, she no more than glanced at the people in the wide entrance foyer, but went directly to the floor on which her audition had been scheduled. A monitor seated at a small desk greeted her pleasantly and checked her name against his list.

"The voice tests are running late," he told her. "Would you like to warm up for a while?"

"Oh, I would!" Julie had hoped there would be a chance to do this.

Alone in a small practice room, she concentrated on vocalizing, but not for long. Her watch might have stopped. They might not call her. In any case she had better be on hand.

She need not have rushed. The two candidates scheduled ahead of her, a boy and a girl, were still waiting in the corridor outside the studio. The boy hailed her.

"Come and join the nervous breakdown society. No charge at all."

"Thank you." Julie sat down beside them.

"This is Liz," the boy said. "I'm Tony. Who're you?"

Julie told them her name and Liz smiled wanly. "Tony'll

probably call you Jule. We've only known each other a few minutes and already we're on a nickname basis."

Tony grinned. "Natch. There's nothing like common misery for starting a beautiful friendship."

"I know what you mean!" Julie said and indeed she at once felt at home with this blond boy and his fidgety chatter, and the plump red-faced girl who sat with her feet so firmly planted on the floor and her hands folded tightly over her music.

The door of the studio opened. As if on a pivot, the three heads turned toward the pale stricken girl who emerged.

"How was it?" Tony asked.

"Awful!" The girl glanced back at the now closed door as if pursued. "I couldn't have passed. I couldn't! I was so scared I fell apart."

"Sure you passed. Take it easy." Tony gave the harassed girl a pat and then threw out his hands and raised his eyes to heaven. "I should talk. I'm next."

The girl burst into tears and fled.

Tony whistled, "Whew!" Liz grew stiffer. Julie pulled out a handkerchief and wiped the perspiration from her hands and forehead. Don't you get scared, she admonished herself. Don't get scared!

And when at last her turn came and she stood beside the piano in the big studio, she was not scared. She was numb.

The judges sat at a long table. There must be ten of

them, ten pairs of eyes boring into her, ten pencils poised to seal her fate. They asked her a few questions and she could only hope her answers made sense. Then out of the blue the chairman asked, "What would you like to do first?"

"First? I—a—oh, *Tu Lo Sai*." Julie had given the chairman a list of the numbers she was prepared to sing, but had not expected to be allowed a choice. She was so flustered that the first chords of the accompanist's introduction seemed like a sound from another world.

But it was a familiar world. She had lived with this music night and day, had heard it rising along the Signora's keyboard and her own, had played the Pinza recording over and over; it had run silently through her head, hour after hour. She reacted as automatically as a knee to the whack of a doctor's hand, and at the proper moment her mouth opened and she sang.

For her second selection, the chairman requested Samuel Barber's *A Nun Takes the Veil*. This was the bugbear, for Julie was not adapted to modern music either by voice or temperament. She got through it, though, and technically did a creditable job.

But technique was not enough in this highly competitive test. If only . . . They did! For her last selection they asked for "Rest in the Lord" from Mendelssohn's *Elijah*. This was an aria she loved and she sang it with love. The men and women before her were no longer a jury, only a group of people to whom she gave herself in song.

"Thank you, Miss Brownell."

The chairman's words were a jolt. Julie was not yet out of her aria, not prepared for this brief dismissal. Dazed, she took the music the accompanist handed her. It was over. The test for which she had worked so long was over. She could hardly believe it.

At first she was elated, sure she had done well, but downstairs in the student lounge, comparing notes with Liz and Tony, her confidence wavered.

"Did they ask you for an operatic aria?" Liz wanted to know.

"No, oratorio."

"You're lucky! I had to sing 'Habanera.'"

Why hadn't they asked for her operatic number? Did they think she was not up to it?

"I got a few smiles out of 'em," Tony said facetiously, and Julie, trying to recall their faces, could not be sure of a single expression.

But she must be accepted. She must! If she had longed for Juilliard before, she wanted it more than ever as the day went on. For music echoed along the corridors; in the lounge and in the cafeteria, snatches of shop talk fell upon her ears, and throughout the school there was an atmosphere of oneness, the identity of a shared love and a common goal.

"That was one of the best parts of it," she told Dave on the way home. "I mean, when you have the same interests, you make friends so quickly."

"Yeah. I saw you had made friends," Dave said.

The sharpness of his tone made Julie turn to search his face. All the way up the highway he had listened sympathetically to her chatter about her audition, her sight-reading test and her written examination; about meeting Liz and Tony and eating lunch with them and exchanging addresses. He had shown no sign of objecting. What was the matter with him now?

"You could have met them," she said. "If I'd seen you in the park when the three of us came out, I would have brought them over and introduced them."

"It's not that, Julie. Only—weren't there any other Negroes in that school?"

"Why—why, yes." She had seen them and talked to them but now she was surprised. Not once in the long day had she thought of color. Music had formed the basis of judgment. Were they vocalists, instrumentalists, or budding composers? With whom had they studied? How had they done in their tests?

If she made Juilliard it could always be like that. Or could it? Face it. Face it. Well, she would, later. After she had heard the results of her test, after the prom, maybe not until after commencement.

22

IT WAS HOT IN THE AUDITORIUM. THE SPEAKER DRONED ON and a fly buzzed around Julie's ear. It seemed that this whole week end had consisted of nothing but trying not to squirm. She would have preferred to stay home but could not disappoint her father who had been so eager to have his family along when this midwestern university conferred an honorary degree upon his oldest friend.

Only what a time to be away! It was almost certain that she would not hear from Juilliard within a week of her test, still their letter might be there right now. Or Dave might hear from his scholarship exam. Besides, she hated to miss sharing anticipation of the prom with her friends. It was to be held next Friday and the whole senior class was buzzing with talk about dates and gowns and plans for parties after the dance.

"I wish I had a fly swatter," Mrs. Brownell whispered, and Julie repressed a giggle. She could just see Mother chasing a fly in the midst of a commencement address.

The exercises dragged to a close, as did the president's reception, and the Brownells were back in their hotel room, packed and ready to go, two hours before train time. Daddy suggested they go for a walk.

"We haven't had much chance to see the city," he said.

"My feet wouldn't carry me another step," Mrs. Brownell protested. "You and Julie go."

"Be fun," Julie said though she wished she had not packed her flat-heeled shoes. The morning's tour of the campus and the long reception had worn out her feet too.

There were not many people on the streets, for most of the Saturday shoppers had gone home and the evening pleasure seekers were not yet abroad. Julie, chatting with Daddy, looking into the store windows paid scant attention to the passers-by and so, at first, the face of the dark-haired young woman did not register. A small part of her mind noticed the smart little hat, and without conscious thought, her eyes slid toward the woman's pretty companion. Slid and snapped back. The dark-haired girl was Lorraine Hall.

Julie stopped in the middle of a sentence, her face alight with happy recognition. Lorraine looked directly at her but there was no answering smile, not the slightest pause in her pace. She passed so close they could have reached out and touched her.

Julie was as stunned as if she had been slapped hard, and she tightened her grip on her father's arm. He covered her hand with his own.

"It wasn't personal, Julie. She couldn't have done anything else."

"But she was my friend!" Julie cried.

"I know. But I'm sure it was harder for her than for us. To see old friends—faces from home . . . Do you realize what it must mean to be completely cut off?"

"But what if I had been Marilyn? What if Marilyn had been the one to see her?"

"Let's just be glad she wasn't," Dr. Brownell said. "And I wouldn't tell her about it, either."

Julie could not get the incident out of her mind and that night in her sleeper berth she relived it in painful detail. It was all much clearer than at the shocked moment of occurrence, and she could see both Lorraine and her friend as she had not in the afternoon. An attractive girl, that friend, well dressed and aristocratic looking, like Beverly Blake.

Why had she thought of Bev, the one who had almost but never wholly accepted her, before whom no talent, no effort at friendliness could disguise the color of a person's skin?

Disguise? Julie could no longer put off facing Dave's accusation. Why had she been embarrassed by the discussions of race prejudice? Why had she been disturbed when Rickie had spoken to her as a Negro, or whenever Bev had gone to the opposite extreme? Had she actually been trying like Lorraine, to deny her race?

These questions formed an undertone to the excitement of the next week, sometimes rising to a crescendo but often fading away, like the minor accompaniment to a song. They were not there in the ecstatic moment when she was notified of her acceptance by Juilliard. They were not there when Dave phoned to tell her he had won his scholarship. They were not there, at first, when Marilyn dropped her bomb and announced that she was engaged to be married to George.

"Married!" Julie was astounded. To her, marriage was part of a very distant future.

"You don't need to act so horrified." Marilyn's eyes twinkled. "It's a perfectly respectable institution."

"Oh, I'm not," Julie assured her. "Only it's such a surprise. I didn't think George . . . Why, Marilyn, you'll practically be my cousin."

"I know it," Marilyn said happily. "It's going to be wonderful, Julie. George is going back to his father's store and some day it'll be his. Ours. I'll go on working but not for long. My brothers are getting old enough to help, and anyway, George wants to take care of me."

Yes, George would. Marilyn, struggling to help her family, must have appealed to his one soft spot, his protectiveness. But Julie wondered how long he would stick it out, whether his pattern of defeat was not so firmly fixed that he would soon slip back into it and Marilyn would go on leading very much the dreary life she always had.

And now it was not a question that troubled Julie. It was a sure awareness that she might have helped George before it was too late. Four years ago she, too, had aroused her cousin's best instincts and had let them die, had shunned him to seek a place in a more desirable world.

Well, she had won that place, and no act on her part could change it now, not with so little time left before the end of school. Besides, she had not only won it, she had earned it and she was not going to let worry spoil these last few weeks, especially the biggest night of all, the prom.

For this occasion, George broke all precedent and at Marilyn's request agreed to go.

"I don't know what I'll wear," Marilyn told Julie, "but at least I'll be there."

"I'll lend you a dress," Julie said. "How about my light-blue taffeta?"

"Your blue taffeta! Oh, Julie! Will it fit?"

It did not quite fit but when Mrs. Brownell had taken in the seams, it looked as if it had been made for Marilyn.

Julie's dress was white with a fitted bodice and miles and miles of tulle skirt. She felt right in it, glamorous almost, and when she went down to meet Dave, with his corsage fastened to her wrist, it was as if she were making an entrance. Daddy and Mother, Sarah Lou and Dave all stood at the foot of the stairs watching her and she walked slowly to savor this moment to the full.

Daddy's love, his delight in her, showed in his face. "You look lovely, Julie. I'd like to be taking you to that dance myself."

"Thank you, Daddy." Julie spoke appreciatively, but when she turned to Dave, so handsome in his white jacket and dark tie and trousers, her tone switched to banter. "I already have a date."

Mother pretended to be annoyed. "Well! All this certainly leaves me out!"

Daddy's answer was to put his arm around her shoulders and Julie, viewing them from her high peak of happiness, rushed over and planted a lipsticky kiss on each of their foreheads.

"Now who's left out?" Dave complained and Julie said, "You wait. Your turn comes later."

The dance was held in the ballroom of a hotel. Julie was more than ever pleased with her dress when she saw how well it looked with the decorations. Rich red curtains hung at the long windows and the bandstand was banked with masses of white flowers. Small tables had been placed along the walls and on each there was one red rosebud.

Julie and Dave sat between Marilyn and George on one side and Anna and Rickie on the other—that is, except when they danced, swinging through the fast numbers and gliding dreamily through the slow ones. Dave had improved a great deal as a dancer. He had always had rhythm and grace but not this finished smoothness.

Shortly before the intermission, Bill Manny entertained them with a few songs. Everyone stood around the platform to listen, packed as tightly together as if the whole ballroom were not stretched out behind them. He had finished and the crowd had started to move away when someone yelled, "Hey! Let's have a song from Julie Brownell."

Others took up the cry and in the hubbub, Julie could only question Dave with her eyes. He smiled encouragement and broke a path for her through the crowd to the platform.

Bill Manny had returned to the piano and he asked her what she wanted to sing.

"Oh, I don't know." Julie turned to her classmates. "What would you like to hear?"

Several people called out the names of popular songs and one fellow shouted, "Sing that opera."

"Naw!" someone else retorted. "Who wants culture on a night like this?"

Bill Manny threw out a feeler, softly strumming the melody of a popular tune. He looked to Julie for confirmation and she nodded assent and sang his selection.

The applause called for an encore. Julie smiled at her classmates, her eyes moving from one to the other until they rested on Dave. He looked so alone. All the others stood close to their dates, shoulders touching, arms linked or hands joined. With a flash of compassion, she saw his aloneness as more than the separation of space between them. Dave stood alone because his girl was not with him in spirit, because she had never truly taken a stand beside her race.

She leaned across the piano and spoke to Bill Manny. "Can you play *Swing Low, Sweet Chariot*?"

"Yes, ma'am," Bill said. "Yes, ma'am."

When she heard the first notes, Julie was seized by a

moment of wild regret. Why had she chosen at the last to point up what she had so nearly managed to hide, that Julie Brownell was different from the rest? Someone turned out the lights and directed the spotlight to where she stood, a dark dark girl in a pure-white dress. She stepped forward and clasped her hands.

"*Swing Low, Sweet Chario—ot.* . . ." Suddenly, miraculously, the turmoil was gone. The darkened room, her classmates, the band playing its soft accompaniment behind her, all became a part of the song. Her song. The song of her people. It was almost as if she were not Julie Brownell but instead all those who had suffered before her; all those yet to come.

The last note died away. There was not a movement, not a breath in the entire ballroom. Then the lights went up and the applause broke around her, a triumphant thunder in her ears.

Spontaneously, Bill and his band crashed into *All God's Chillun Got Shoes.* This time Julie motioned to her classmates to join her and they did. Their feet tapped to the beat, their shoulders swung, and their voices were raised as one with hers. When it was finished she waved to them once and walked across the platform and down the steps to Dave.

"Julie . . ." he started, but he did not stand a chance, not with everyone crowding around her.

Rickie got there first. "Don't do that often," he said. "You had my girl in tears. All over my clean hankie, too."

He shook the crumpled handkerchief at Anna's laughing face.

Johnny Trent came next, his head waggling in wonderment. "Boy!" he said. "Can you chirp!"

Bev Blake was natural and relaxed. "You were simply super, Julie. Only a Negro can make spirituals sound right."

Doris Regan—pathetically, Julie thought—tried too late to get into the act. "To think that we used to make mud pies together. David, I knew Julie when."

Only George was displeased. "Julie, did you have to . . ."

Marilyn cut him off. "Come on, Georgie. The band's starting. Let's dance."

As others began dancing, Dave pulled Julie across the ballroom toward the door. Just before they went out they passed Bets Hampton who smiled, but in such a supercilious way that Julie's old resentment flared up. Flared up and died down. There would always be Bets Hamptons and she must learn to take them in her stride.

Out on the terrace there were only Dave and herself and the sound of distant music and the sight of a billion stars.

"Julie . . ." Dave waited to get the choke out of his voice. "Julie, you win. I'll break down those doors but you will lead the people through."

As a symbol of his faith, at last, at last, he gave her his ring. It was too big for her finger and she had no chain so he tied it around her neck with a lace from his shoe.

Julie laughed softly. "How're you going to dance?"

Dave did not answer. He couldn't very well talk when he was kissing his girl. But when they started back to the ballroom he said, "You look taller all of a sudden."

"It's because I'm holding up my head. I don't want my chin to hide the ring."

Her answer satisfied Dave but it was only partly the truth. Julie looked taller because she felt taller. She had made Negro a word of pride.